Fifth Generation Cowboy

LIZ ISAACSON

"I will instruct thee and teach thee in the way which thou shall go: I will guide thee with mine eye."
~Psalms 32:8

Chapter One

The fences containing Rose Reyes's patience had never seemed so flat. Of course, she hadn't pushed her daughter, Mari, as far out of her comfort zone as she had these past few months.

As she listened to Mari wail over the fact that her cucumbers had touched her ranch dressing before she was ready, Rose sent a prayer for someone, anyone, to come fix the fence line.

Someone.

Anyone.

No one came.

No one ever did.

So Rose sat next to Mari and took a deep breath. "Mari, you need to calm down. When you're ready, I'll be back." She got up and purposely moved down the hall to her bedroom. Even with the door closed, she could hear Mari's hiccups and continued sniffles.

She was safe. She was fine. She just resisted change of any kind, and having cucumbers instead of carrots had already thrown her for a loop.

Scratching came against Rose's door, and she cracked it to let in Paprika, the little shih tzu that could usually settle Mari. Now, Rose picked up the dog and stroked her head, taking the animal's latent energy as her own.

Mari had been having more episodes lately, something Doctor Parchman had predicted. The therapist at Courage Reins, the riding center where Mari participated in equine therapy a couple times a week, had sent Rose home with some brochures about how to deal with the outbursts, and Rose met with Doctor Parchman once a month to make sure she worked with Mari appropriately at home.

She'd done the best she could, but Mari's continued crying would've challenged Mother Teresa. Rose sighed and gazed out the window, glad Mari had another riding appointment that evening.

That is, if Rose could get Mari calm enough to finish eating and get in the car. The silence beyond the door snagged Rose's attention and she took Paprika with her as she rejoined Mari in the kitchen.

Half the grilled cheese sandwich was gone. But the cucumbers were still stubbornly pushed to the side, the smudge of white on the corner of an innocent vegetable the culprit of Mari's outburst.

"Feel better?" Rose asked her daughter, smoothing the girl's bangs off her forehead.

Mari didn't answer, a typical response. Rose turned away, her usual reaction. Mostly so Mari wouldn't accidentally see Rose's frustration, the tears that settled in the corners of her eyes. Rose never wanted Mari to know she longed to have a real conversation with someone—someone who didn't need a line of credit, a construction loan, or an extension on their due date.

As the loan manager at Three Rivers Bank, the only adults Rose spoke with had the same problems she did. Some worse. Some easier. But she knew better than most that everybody had problems.

Hers weren't financial, and as Mari put her plate—still laden with the dreaded cucumbers—in the sink, a tidal wave of guilt nearly sent Rose to her knees. Guilt that she wanted someone to talk to that would talk back. Guilt that she counted her own daughter as a problem. Guilt that she felt so downtrodden when she knew others had it worse than she did.

"Ready to go riding?" she asked, forcing back the tears and a measure of brightness into her voice.

Mari made eye contact for less than a blink. "Okay."

"Okay, then." Rose smiled. "Go get changed. We'll be late if we wait much longer."

While Mari changed out of her school clothes and into her riding pants, Rose checked her phone to make sure it had enough charge to get to the ranch and back. With summer still a couple months off, darkness came early, and the last thing she wanted was to be stranded on the lonely stretch of road between town and the ranch without a way to call for help.

By the time Mari returned, Rose had her jacket and cowgirl hat waiting. They were ten minutes late leaving, but she knew better than to rush the girl. Rose spent most of her life waiting for Mari, and she'd learned to start tasks thirty minutes early so Mari could finish them on time.

"Let's go," Rose said, swiping her keys from the kitchen counter, where her empty dinner plate still sat.

She called Tom Lovell, the cowboy who usually worked with Mari at the facility, a stone in her stomach. She hated telling him they'd be late, though he never acted like it mattered. Still, she knew time was valuable, and someone with as many responsibilities as Tom surely couldn't afford to be sitting around.

"Rose," he said, his friendly voice a welcome addition to Rose's life.

"Hello, Tom," she said, wondering if he was as happy to hear her voice as she was his. Probably not. He had plenty of adults to converse with throughout the day.

"We're just leaving, so we'll be a tiny bit late." She backed out of the driveway as she held down the button for the garage door. It wouldn't budge. She braked, stopped, and tried again.

Nothing.

"No problem," Tom drawled as Rose put the car in park. Impatience really wanted to win over her today, but she tamped down the frustration as she reached for the rope and pulled the door down manually.

A loud screech accompanied her words when she said, "And if you have any of that dark roast coffee on, I'd love a cup when I get there."

He chuckled. "Rough day?"

Rose basked in the warmth of his laugh, slightly embarrassed at her reaction to him, though he wasn't there and couldn't see her.

"You could say that," she said. "Be there soon."

"I'll start the coffee for you."

Rose hung up, tucked her phone in her jacket pocket, and settled back into the driver's seat with a moan.

Halfway to the ranch, her phone rang. She checked it and saw the name Ed. She thumbed the call to voicemail, unwilling to add to the weight of today with a conversation with her ex-husband. He could at least wait until after the session.

"Dad," Mari said, pointing at the still flashing screen.

"We'll call him back after you ride Peony." Rose added a smile to the end of her statement.

"Peony," Mari echoed.

"That's right." Rose patted Mari's leg and kept on toward Three Rivers. She pulled into the parking lot at Courage Reins and exhaled as Mari got out of the car without prompting. She'd gotten better at a lot of things since starting the equine therapy eighteen months ago, including her schoolwork, talking to her teachers, and becoming more independent.

But apparently, not eating cucumbers.

Rose allowed herself a small smile as a burden lifted from her shoulders. She should've focused on where Mari had improved instead of wallowing in the negative.

"Tomorrow's another day," she told herself. "And Mari will be—"

"You gettin' out?" Tom leaned into the passenger door, bending his tall frame down to look at her under the brim of his cowboy hat.

Rose startled and her face heated when she thought of him listening to her talk to herself.

"Yes. Yeah, I'm getting out." She fumbled with the door handle and managed to free herself from the vehicle. She straightened and met Tom's eye over the roof of her sedan.

"Hey." She peered past him toward the riding ring. "You see which way Mari went?"

"She ran like the wind toward the barn." He nodded back behind Rose. "I've got your coffee on." He gestured toward the house a hundred yards from the parking lot. "Well, Chelsea's got your coffee on." He gave her a lazy smile, and she couldn't help returning it.

"Thanks, Tom." She glanced over her shoulder to the barn. "You think…?"

"She'll be fine. Pete's with her." Tom started walking toward the house.

"You usually train with her," Rose said, hating the worried shiver in her tone. "She's…she's been having a hard time lately."

"Not out here." Tom stepped closer to her, and Rose almost tripped though the dirt road was fairly smooth. "Give yourself a break," he said. "You sounded pretty tired on the phone."

"Oh, great," Rose said. "That's just what I want to hear." She nudged him with her elbow. "Do I look terrible too?"

"'Course not." Tom stuffed his hat lower over his eyes so she couldn't see them. She didn't have to look at him to know he had the darkest pair of midnight eyes. Beautiful, midnight eyes she could lose herself in if she wasn't careful. And if Rose had learned one thing, it was not to get suckered in by a beautiful pair of midnight eyes.

Yet somehow she still found herself thinking of Tom and his

calm, steady manner whenever she contemplated the type of man she'd like to marry one day.

One day in the far future, she told herself as Tom ushered her through Pete and Chelsea's back fence and into the yard.

One thing Rose knew, she wouldn't remarry until Mari was an adult and able to take care of herself. Still, Rose cast a longing glance at Tom, wondering what had kept the handsome cowboy from getting snatched up.

Tom's phone buzzed as he reached the sliding glass door. He checked the text and saw Chelsea's name. *Julie's fussing. I'll be upstairs if you need me.*

He refrained from rolling his eyes. His dad said if he did it too often, his eyes might get stuck that way. But the only adequate reaction to a text like Chelsea's was an eyeroll. See, the woman thought Tom needed to spend time alone with Rose. Then he'd be able to ask her out.

Even though Tom had repeatedly told her, and her husband Pete, and everyone else who ribbed him about his friendship with Rose, that he and Rose were only friends. The cowhands had given him copious amounts of unwanted advice for how to ask her out, and he'd given them enough eyerolls to be in danger of his eyes getting stuck.

Chelsea had been texting Kelly for three solid months about how they could get Tom a date. Even Kate, Brett's wife, had spent hours of her time trying to get him to take out one of his friends.

He'd tried with Tammy, and that had ended after the first date. Mutually, but Tom hadn't been able to go back to the sports bar yet, and it had been months since they attended the hay festival together.

And for the past several weeks now, Tom had spent more than a healthy amount of time assuring everyone he wasn't romantically interested in the gorgeous Rose Reyes.

Much as he wished she wouldn't, Desi, his ex-girlfriend, popped into his mind. She seemed to be haunting him for the past month, always whispering to him that his cool demeanor toward women was as attractive as it was maddening. After their break-up a few years ago, Tom hadn't really tried to find another woman.

Rose exhaled heavily, bringing him back to the warmth of Pete and Chelsea's kitchen. Rose rubbed her hands together and sat down at the bar. "I don't think I've ever been in Chelsea's house. It's nice."

"Yeah, real nice." Tom lifted the coffee pot and poured a mug for Rose. He passed it to her and prepared one for himself. "Cream and sugar right there."

Rose flashed him a grateful smile as she doctored up her coffee while he slid onto the stool next to her.

Tom sipped the dark brew, wishing he could think of something to say. He wasn't particularly skilled with conversation, having grown up with an older brother and raised by a single dad after his mom went to work one day and never came home. Tom had been seven, and he hadn't had a lot of women in his life since. Hadn't needed them, hadn't wanted them.

He glanced at Rose, at the dark caramel color of her skin, her deep brown eyes, her long hair the color of Houdini's coat. Tom inwardly cringed at his comparison of this woman to a black quarter horse.

He cleared his throat. "So what's been goin' on with Mari?"

"She…" Rose waved her free hand toward the sink. "She has Autism."

Tom studied her, trying to find the root of her unhappiness. "Yeah, and?"

"And, I don't know." She looked at him and glanced away quickly. "Can I tell you a secret?"

Tom's nerves buzzed and his skin felt too hot. "Sure, of course."

"You won't judge me?"

"I would never judge you." Tom spoke with all the sincerity of his heart.

Her earnest expression caused him to lean closer. The way she'd asked for coffee earlier had alerted him to her distress. As soon as she'd hung up, he'd hurried over to Pete's to see if he could take over Mari's therapy.

"You're a jumpy as a wet cat," Pete had said. "When are you gonna ask that woman out?"

Tom hadn't known how to answer. For the first time in all the months of teasing he'd endured, he'd never once considered Rose as more than a friend. But with Pete's question, he hadn't been prompted to roll his eyes and heave a sigh of exasperation.

Rose took a deep breath. "Okay, well, sometimes taking care of Mari is exhausting. I love her, don't get me wrong, but she isn't exactly chatty, and sometimes I just want someone to talk to. She's been more emotional these past few months, and I know the therapist said that would be normal, but I'm going crazy." She gave a little chuckle that sounded anything but happy.

"She's going with her dad tomorrow, and I'll admit that I'm really looking forward to her being gone." She clapped her hand over her mouth, her eyes wide.

Tom blinked in sync with Rose. He reached for her hands and gently lowered them from her face. "Rose." Emotion laced the way he said her name. "You're a great mom."

She squeezed his fingers, and he stared at their entwined hands, adrenaline racing through his system. He released her like he'd been electrocuted, shocked at the heat rising from his stomach. Heat from touching *Rose*.

"I feel like a failure," she said, tucking her hands around her coffee cup. "Sometimes we just eat cereal for dinner. And my yard is a mess, and the kitchen sink leaks, and most of the time I barely feel like I've got my head above water."

Tom lowered his chin so he couldn't see Rose, so he could work through these new, confusing feelings. "I can come help with the plumbing," he said real low, the words barely escaping his throat. "You takin' her to Amarillo or is Ed coming to get her?"

"He's coming."

Tom took a hot gulp of his coffee, trying to get his stomach to settle. "Great. I'll come over in the morning."

"You don't need—"

"Rose." He took a breath and looked up, right into her eyes. "I want to."

Thankfully, she didn't argue. Just nodded and took his phone to put in her address. When he took it back, he glanced at where her hands had been, a slow smile spreading his lips.

"You're acting like fixing my pipes is going to be a picnic," Rose teased.

"You volunteering to feed me lunch?" He grinned at her, hoping she'd say yes.

She did, and by the time she left, Tom knew he wouldn't be able to sleep that night, excited as he was to fix a set of leaking pipes—or was he looking forward to seeing Rose again?

Confusion would definitely keep him awake tonight too.

The next morning, he wrangled Ethan out of bed just before dawn. "Come on, cowboy." Tom nudged Ethan's foot. "You said you'd cover chores for me this morning."

"Didn't say nothin' about gettin' up at dawn."

"That's what the morning chores are. Come on. I have an hour, and then I have to go."

Ethan muttered under his breath, but he got up and pulled on a pair of jeans. Tom retreated from the bunks to the kitchenette, where he started a pot of coffee. A few minutes later, a more alert Ethan joined him.

The cowhand had come out to Three Rivers a couple of years ago, and though he had a mouth on him, he was a hard worker. He mussed his blond hair as he yawned. "You so owe me for this."

"You're getting paid," Tom said. "And earning hours toward another day off."

Ethan reached for a piece of bread and set it in the toaster. "That's the only reason I agreed to this." While he waited for the bread to brown, he pulled on a heavy jacket. "Where you goin', anyway?"

Tom checked the coffee maker, hoping for nonchalance. "I have some business in town."

"Business with Rose Reyes." The toast popped up and Ethan turned to butter it. "I didn't know the bank was open on Saturday."

Tom opted not to answer, instead taking a clean mug out of the cupboard and pouring himself a cup of coffee. "I'll start in the barn."

Ethan wouldn't like that, but Tom didn't care much. He'd agreed to this morning's chores; Tom didn't have to help him at all. But he couldn't sleep past five, used as he was to getting up and getting things done around the ranch.

He arrived in the barn quickly, but then slowed his pace. Wandering through the aisles, acknowledging the horses as they came to their gates for his morning greeting. He paused at Peony's stall, the gentle creature nuzzling him with her warm nose.

"Hey, girl." He gave her an affectionate pat before continuing down the line. Houdini, Tom's favored horse, nickered a hello.

Tom grinned at him and leaned against his railing. "Morning to you too, Dini." A working horse, Houdini liked going out in the cool mornings the way Tom did. Houdini was more wild than the other horses Tom had taken a shine to, but loyal and strong.

He seemed to know when weekends came 'round, because he nudged Tom's shoulder with his nose before retreating in his stall for another doze.

That was Tom's cue to get to work. He went down the line, filling water troughs and hay bins. He checked on Iris, the pregnant mare due to give birth in another month or so. He made her stand so he could rake out her straw before giving her a fresh bed.

"There you go," he told her, a stream of satisfaction bubbling beneath his skin when she settled down and went right back to sleep.

Peace descended on Tom as he cut through the cold morning to his cabin. He loved the hard, physical labor of ranching. It reminded him of what had always been solid in his life, what never left, never changed.

He showered, his mind revolving around the mother he hadn't spoken to for two decades. He wondered if she ever thought about him. If she remembered his birthday. If she knew how deep her actions had sliced.

Tom's father never spoke of his wife. Tom didn't know if they'd gotten divorced or not. His dad had never remarried, choosing instead to dedicate his life to his boys and the ranch he ran.

As Tom scrubbed the stink of horse from his hair, he understood his father on a deeper level. Fear frothed up with the soap as he thought about his reaction to touching Rose's hands. Did he really want a woman in his life? One who could up and leave at any given moment, without a phone call, a hug good-bye?

He leaned his head back and let the spray hit his throat,

frustrated that his mother affected him so strongly, after so many years.

Tom's cell phone rang, sending his heart into his throat. Maybe Rose needed to cancel. As his pulse settled, he thought he might just be able to say he hadn't gotten her message.

He stepped out of the shower, toweled off, and went into his bedroom. A blue light flashed on his phone, and he hesitated before swiping it on. Eventually, he did, only to find a missed call from his older brother, Jace.

As if his circular thoughts about their mother had summoned the call. Tom smiled at the screen. No message. His brother never left one. He had more to say than Tom, but he rarely did it on a recording.

Tom called him back while he pulled out a fresh pair of jeans.

"Jace," he said when his brother picked up on the second ring. "It's early."

"I know, I remembered that after the phone started ringing. Sorry."

"I was up. In the shower."

"I just got back from my morning chores."

Tom set the phone on speaker and started getting dressed. "So, what's goin' on?" Jace worked the ranch where they'd grown up, after a brief stint of trying college. Wasn't for him, he claimed, and he'd gone back to Montana and started working for their father.

Tom had tried the Army, and when that didn't work out, he had nowhere else to go. His father knew a couple of ranchers down here, so Tom moved south. He'd bounced from ranch to ranch for a year or two before finally settling at Three Rivers.

"Dad fell last night," Jace said, and everything in Tom's world stalled. His voice couldn't seem to battle its way to the surface.

"It wasn't bad," Jace added. "But I took him to the hospital anyway. He has a foot fracture."

Tom thought of his tall, strong father. No way he'd stay off that foot. "No cast?"

"No cast." Jace sighed. "I'm sure you know what that means."

"He was out doing chores this morning too."

"Yep." Jace chuckled, and the concerned sound echoed through the line, assaulting Tom's ears. "Anyway, I wanted you to know. Maybe you can put his name on your church's prayer roll or something."

Tom didn't come from a religious family. His father lived, breathed, and worked a cattle ranch. He claimed he didn't have time for organized religion, but he'd taken Tom and Jace to services on Christmas and Easter.

When Tom had come to Texas, he'd enjoyed his Sundays at church more than he thought he would. Jace leaned more toward their father's side of the line, but he respected Tom and his beliefs.

"Sure thing, Jace." He hesitated, not quite sure what else to say.

"And one note of good news," Jace said, a smile infusing his voice. "You know how I've been saving for that diamond ring?"

"Yeah."

"I finally have enough. I'm gonna ask Wendy to marry me."

Tom's throat tightened and released. His brother didn't seem to have any of Tom's anxiety over women and marriage. "When?"

"I don't know. Soon, I think. I need to make a plan."

Tom heard his father's words in Jace's, and he wondered if sometimes he and Jace planned too much. Rose's face danced through his mind's eye, and Tom realized why he hadn't seen her standing right in front of him.

He had no plan. No plan to find a woman and marry her. No plan to look at Rose as anything but what she already was: His friend.

Had everyone else seen something between them he hadn't? His fingers tingled, as if reminding him of how soft her skin had been.

"Good luck," he told his brother, telling himself the same thing. He whistled as he brushed his teeth and donned his cowboy hat. He had no idea if something could exist between him and Rose. Didn't even know if he *wanted* something to exist between them. But Tom Lovell knew one thing: He didn't want to miss someone standing right in front of him because he was too busy being a horseman.

Chapter Two

Rose woke early, the weight of a normal work day absent. She smiled into the faint dawn light, a weekend of relaxation on the horizon. Mari wouldn't be up for at least an hour, so Rose stayed snuggled under the blankets for another thirty minutes. She padded into the kitchen to make coffee, remembering that Tom would be coming that morning.

She glanced around the kitchen and attached dining room, noting the piles of mail she hadn't opened, Mari's school papers, the dinner dishes from last night, the jackets, bags, and shoes.

Tom couldn't come here and see this. She tossed the instant coffee granules into the machine and began cleaning, the earlier relaxation gone. Her chest felt tight as the minutes ticked by, as Mari got up and demanded scrambled eggs, and Rose had to take precious time to pack her daughter's overnight bag.

Ed arrived at nine-thirty, right on time, as always. Mari let him in, smiled as she stooped for her suitcase.

"Rose," Ed said, nodding in her direction. The only adult she should be confessing to, and he wasn't interested. A pinch started behind her eyes.

"Good morning, Ed." Always the puppet, Rose put on her happy face and stepped toward her ex to give him a quick hug. "She's been really emotional this week," she whispered into Ed's shoulder.

"I'll watch her," Ed promised, stepping back and taking Mari's bag. "And I need to talk to you when I drop her off on Sunday."

"Sure, okay," Rose said, putting her hands in the pockets of her robe and retreating several paces away. "What about?"

He glanced at Mari, his dark eyes filled with concern. With secrets. "I need to talk to you in private."

Rose nodded, her insides snarling. Private for Ed meant something with his girlfriend. Had he proposed? Had the woman met Mari? She'd said nothing about another woman at her dad's, but then again, Mari didn't talk a whole lot about anything besides Peony and Paprika.

"Have fun, baby." Rose squeezed Mari's shoulder and watched her walk out the door with Ed. She leaned in the doorjamb as they climbed in Ed's truck and he backed out of the driveway.

Rose let her eyes linger on the overgrown shrubs lining the front walk, the grass that needed to be cut, aerated, and fertilized. The old basketball hoop with rust and without a basket. The exterior that needed a fresh coat of paint. Maybe two.

As she stood realizing the pathetic condition of her house, another truck pulled into her driveway.

Tom.

Panic poured through Rose as she spun away from the doorway. She wasn't even dressed!

"Mornin'," Tom's voice came from outside. Great. He'd already seen her.

She poked her head around the corner, combing her fingers through her hair. "Come on in," she said. "Mari just left. I have to run and get dressed."

She practically sprinted away from the door and down the hall, slamming the door behind her and punching the lock with her thumb. Not that she thought Tom would barge into her bedroom while she was changing, but still. She felt safer with the door locked.

She pressed her back into the door and took a deep, deep breath. She would've liked to have showered, but that possibility had fled. She applied copious amounts of deodorant and put on a comfortable pair of working pants and an old striped sweatshirt. She immediately yanked the baggy shirt off and selected a more fitted, apricot colored blouse.

Rose ducked into the bathroom and brushed her teeth and tried to tame her hair into submission. It halfway complied, and she swiped on a layer of pink lip gloss before stepping into the kitchen.

"Sorry," she said. "The morning got away from me."

Tom turned from where he stood at the kitchen sink, gazing out the window and into the backyard. He scanned her quickly, a smile curving his lips.

Something sparked in Rose's core, and she suddenly realized why she was so nervous for him to arrive. And it wasn't because she was embarrassed about the condition of her house. Well, maybe a little.

But now, she drank in the tall form of the man before her. He wore a pair of clean jeans, his cowboy boots, and a brown leather jacket. And that delicious cowboy hat, which he tipped to her as he said, "No problem."

"Coffee?" She lunged toward the pot and seized it like it could be a shield between her and her new realization that she had actual feelings for Tom Lovell. Her mind flew to Mari, and the tremors in her hands calmed.

There could be nothing between her and this handsome cowboy. Not for another ten years, at least.

Besides, he was practically her only friend, and she didn't want things to be weird between them.

She poured them both a cup of coffee, adding a bit more cream and sugar to hers than she normally did. "So I didn't quite have time to clean out underneath the sink." She opened the garage door and retrieved an old bucket from the counter that ran the length of the wall.

When she returned to the kitchen, Tom had opened the cabinet under the sink. "Uh, Rose?"

She joined him and knelt. He didn't need to say anything more. "Oh, no." Rose moaned as she began plucking bottles of painkiller and empty vases from the muck on the bottom of the cabinet. "I guess this has been leaking more than I thought."

"The whole thing needs to be replaced." Tom grabbed the dish soap and tossed it into the sink. Between the two of them, it only took a few minutes to empty the cabinet. Tom swiped off his cowboy hat and ducked underneath the sink.

He whistled a low warning. "Rose, this is bad."

She sat back on her heels. "Can you fix it?"

He emerged from the cabinet, and water dripped from his chin. He wiped it while Rose took in his head of dark hair.

"I don't think I've ever seen you without your hat." Rose's voice held an awed quality, and Tom's eyes found hers and locked.

The right side of his mouth kicked into a smile and he ran wet fingers through damp hair. "Can I have my hat back?"

Rose startled when she realized she had his hat gripped in both her hands. Mutely, because she couldn't think of anything to say, she extended it toward him.

Rose stood on the edge of the patio in her backyard, her skin prickling all over like someone was watching her. Someone was. Tom Lovell. From the dining room window.

She ignored him, the same way she was trying to ignore the lava flowing through her veins. How had Tom rendered her speechless after all these months? Maybe this spark had always existed between them and she'd just never felt it until now because of everything happening at work, with Ed dating again, with Mari's new schedule. Or perhaps Rose had never let herself look at Tom as anything more than the cowhand who helped her daughter, or the friend who greeted her when she showed up at Three Rivers.

But last night he'd made her coffee, sat with her while she talked, actually listened. He'd been her friend.

Of course we're friends, she chastised herself while she waited for

Paprika to take care of her business. *We've known each other for almost two years.*

Rose had admired his solid strength, his dependability, his midnight eyes. But she'd never reacted to him the way she just had.

She toed the dirt Mari liked to draw in when it was her turn to take out Paprika, wondering what she should do. Surely Tom had noticed a change too. A charge that strong couldn't be missed.

She glanced over her shoulder, but couldn't see him. "Come on, Paprika," she called, suddenly anxious to get back in the house, back to Tom, so she could find out what was really going on between them.

"Probably nothing," she told herself as the little dog came bounding out of the weeds. Rose watched the tall tops of them settle back into stillness, really seeing for the first time how long it had been since she'd done any yard work.

With a heavy sigh, she scooped up Paprika and went back to the more immediate problem: Tom.

Oh, and the broken kitchen sink.

"Rose, this is gonna cost a couple hundred dollars." Tom perched on the edge of a barstool, watching her. His muscles felt tight, but a sense of euphoria bled through him. The two sensations warred with each other as he remembered the glint in her expression as she stared at him without his hat.

He'd always felt naked without it, but if she'd look at him like that again, he'd take it off right now.

"That's okay," she said. "I know where to get a loan if I need one." She flashed him a tight smile, but she didn't let her gaze settle on him. She hadn't since handing his hat back, since scampering away from him and dumping the bucket full of her supplies in the garage, since standing in the backyard with her dog for ten minutes. "So I guess we're going to the hardware store?"

Giddiness swept through Tom, making him lightheaded. He thought he'd fix Rose's pipes in a couple of minutes and need to invent a way to kill a couple of hours before their lunch.

But the way that water steadily streamed from the pipes indicated this job was much bigger than a couple of minutes.

"I'll drive," he said as she shouldered her purse.

"Tom." She took a step toward him, finally meeting his eye. "You don't have to...I mean, surely this isn't how you want to spend your Saturday."

"Sure it is," he said easily, glad his voice didn't betray him. "I like fixing things."

She followed him out the front door, where Tom took in the disarray of her yard. Her walls needed paint, her linoleum needed replacing, and an idea needled his mind.

"Don't you ever take a day off?" she asked as she closed the passenger door behind her.

"Yeah," he said. "Sundays." He backed out of her driveway. "Well, sometimes. I do the basic chores on the ranch and that's it. And Garth and I switch off so we both get a day completely off."

"You like ranching?"

"Love it," Tom said without hesitation. "I grew up on a ranch.

27

My daddy was the foreman of the Horseshoe Home Ranch in Montana. I've always been a horseman." He cut her a quick glance to see her reaction. "I'm a fifth generation cowboy. It's a lot of work, but I love it."

She smiled. "I can tell." She slid her eyes his way. "Am I taking you from your work on the ranch today?"

She was, but he waved his hand like it didn't matter. "I've got it covered." Spending the whole day with Rose was worth twice what he'd have to pay Ethan.

"That means yes."

"Rose, I have it covered." Maybe he could ask her to dinner. Maybe use her kitchen as a reason why they needed to go out to eat. His mind churned as forcefully as his stomach as they picked out a new sink, bought replacement pipes, and a new section of kitchen cabinetry.

"It's the wrong color," Rose said, peering at the door as she opened it. "It's nice. But it's not going to match."

"I can stain it."

She peered at him now, her eyes seeing right past the false tone in his voice. "You can stain it? It still won't match the others."

Tom turned his back on her, embarrassed. "We can stain them all. A little kitchen makeover."

Rose circled him, and he admired her tenacity, her straightforward manner, her dark eyes and petite frame. "We?"

Taking a deep breath, taking a step toward her, taking a chance, Tom swept his fingers from her shoulder to her fingers, where he squeezed hers in his. "Yeah. Me and you. You can use a paintbrush, can't you?"

"I guess." She stared at him. "But Tom—"

"No buts, Rose. You need a minor kitchen remodel, and I'm going to help you do it." He stepped over to the cart and started pushing it toward the checkout.

"You can't—"

"I can."

"Tom." Rose grabbed the cart and it swung wildly to the right, where she stood, her chest heaving.

"Rose."

"You are not remodeling my kitchen."

"No, I'm going to help *you* remodel your kitchen."

She shook her head, a determined glint in her eye and a slash of anger on her mouth. "No. I can do it."

Tom studied her, and finally shrugged when she wouldn't relent. "Okay. Let's at least get the stuff you need to re-stain the cabinets. I'll show you how to do it and you can have at it." He swung the cart toward the paint aisle, giving in for now.

But he wasn't giving up completely. Rose needed a lot more work done around her house. He'd just have to make sure it was *her* idea to have *him* help her with it.

"So you just move it back and forth like that." Tom swished the brush up, then down. "Always in the same direction." He finished the stroke and looked at Rose to make sure she understood. "Wanna try?"

She held out her hand for the brush, and he passed it over. The concentration on her face as she dipped it in the stain and wiped the excess against the side pulled at Tom's heartstrings. He wished he'd made her buy a second brush so he could get to work on the other cabinets while she finished the new piece for the sink.

But she'd insisted that she didn't need him helping her. Only a demonstration, nothing more. He watched her swipe the stain onto the wood with precision, much the same way Rose did everything.

Tom stood and moved away from her, his mind reeling with his newfound knowledge about Rose. He'd definitely been observing her for months, knew things about her he didn't know he did, wanted to know a lot more.

It makes sense, he told himself as he ripped open a package of sandpaper. *You've been friends for a while.*

Of course he would know certain things about her, like how she took her coffee, that she was hardly ever on time much as she'd like to be, and that she was precise with nearly everything in her life.

He mused over some possible reasons why Mari would frustrate her. She was unpredictable, imprecise, tardy. Tom rubbed the sandpaper over the door of the cabinet furthest from Rose, his mind scratching much the same way as the paper against the wood.

"Do you like grilled cheese sandwiches?" Rose asked, bringing Tom back to her kitchen, where she now stood over the half stained cabinet.

"Yeah, sure," he said. "Bread and melted cheese. What's not to like?" He grinned at her, a buzzing starting in his gut when she returned the gesture.

"Great. I think I can make that without a sink." She bent down, balanced the paintbrush on the open can of stain, and stepped to the fridge.

Tom continued sanding, a tune his father used to whistle bouncing through his mind. "Does Mari cook?" he asked.

"A little," Rose said. "She'll make herself Ramen noodles or a bagel with cream cheese. She can heat up leftovers in the microwave too, which is nice."

Tom wanted to keep her talking, keep listening to her pretty Texas lilt. "Who takes care of her after school?"

"She has someone who picks her up from the academy and brings her here. They sometimes work on homework, and sometimes they're watching TV when I get home."

"Academy?" Tom asked.

"Yeah, Mari attends a special school on the south end of town. That's why we moved here ten years ago. Loveland Academy is nationally recognized for their work with Autistic students."

Tom finished sanding one cabinet and moved to the next. "I had no idea. Are there a lot of students?"

"It's very small," Rose said. "Another thing I like about it. But a few dozen students come from the nearby areas into Three Rivers. It's the only school between Oklahoma City and Amarillo."

"And you chose to live here over in the city?" he asked.

"I grew up in Dallas." She set buttered bread into a hot skillet and waited while it sizzled. The scent of toasting bread and warm butter teased Tom's nose and made his stomach rumble.

"I love the small town life," Rose continued as she laid slabs of cheese over the bread and topped it with another buttered slice. "It's quieter, less hectic." She shrugged as she searched through a drawer for a spatula. "And I found a job really fast, so we decided this was the best place for us."

"You and Ed decided," Tom stated, his handyman job forgotten. He watched her probe under the sandwiches to see if they'd browned enough and his breath caught somewhere beneath his lungs at her beauty, her grace, her positivity.

"Yeah." She cast him a quick glance. "Ed had a job in Amarillo. He'd go there on Monday morning and come home Friday afternoon."

"What does he do?"

"He's a car guy. Fixes them, restores them, that kind of stuff."

Tom wasn't sure, and maybe the tantalizing aroma of the grilled cheese sandwiches warped her voice, but he thought Rose sounded distant when she spoke of Ed, of their marriage, of his job.

"Maybe he can take a look at your car when he drops Mari off tomorrow." Tom knew the moment the words left his mouth that he'd made a mistake. "I mean—"

"There's nothing wrong with my car." Rose knifed the spatula under one sandwich and flipped it over. She repeated the procedure with the second, her shoulders drooping. "Who am I kidding? It's hanging on by duct tape and a prayer."

Tom chuckled. "I can look at it, if you want."

Rose shook her head. "Not today."

"Next time Mari comes riding," he offered.

Rose speared him with her eyes, and he steadfastly looked back, everything but her forgotten. "I know a thing or two about fixin' a car," he said. "I've worked on a lot of vehicles on the ranch."

Rose finally nodded, turning away from him to get two plates out of the cupboard. But she didn't twist fast enough, and Tom saw the shake in her chin, the sudden glassiness in her eyes.

He wondered how long it had been since someone had offered to help her. Since someone had come by just to talk to her. As he settled down at a rickety dining table to eat with her, he surmised that it had been a long time and that he needed—*wanted*—to remedy that.

"There's something goin' on with this sandwich." Tom took another bite, trying to identify the unique flavor.

"Garlic powder in the butter," Rose said, a small smile of satisfaction slipping across her lips. "You like it?"

He couldn't seem to tear his gaze from hers as he said, "Oh, I like it."

Blooms of pink appeared in her cheeks and she ducked her head, and satisfaction sang through Tom at her reaction.

Chapter Three

Rose nursed a cup of tea while the Texas wind howled outside her window. Tom had left an hour ago, and without him, her world seemed a little emptier. A little darker. A little lonelier.

But Rose liked being alone, had always been an independent soul. That had been one of Ed's complaints, actually. He'd wished they had more common interests, but she'd tried to like traveling to the city for auto shows. But she didn't. She didn't want to drive four hours round trip every weekend, didn't care about carburetors or fuel ratios or horsepower.

With the thought of horsepower, her mind wandered back to the ranch. She'd loved going out there for the past year and a half, loved the sense of purpose it gave to her now she had a concrete way to help Mari.

And Mari had been improving. She spoke more often, and sometimes in longer sentences. Rose could give her directions and have her do them the first time—an anomaly before Mari began riding Peony.

Her cell buzzed and she glanced at the screen. A text from her sister, Fiona, who lived in Amarillo.

Ran into Mari and Ed today at the movies. She's getting so big!

Rose smiled and picked up her phone to text her sister. Her thumbs flew across the screen, but she wasn't fast enough. Fiona texted again before she could finish her message.

Met his fiancée. Yowsers.

Rose's heart stalled mid-beat. The walls seemed to press in on her. Her throat felt hot and sticky.

Fiancée?

Intellectually, Rose knew what the word meant. No wonder he'd wanted to speak with her privately once he brought Mari home.

"Not that it matters," Rose grumbled as she stood and took her teacup into the kitchen. She hadn't finished, but her stomach wasn't playing nice. "He doesn't need my permission to get married again." She stared out the window above the sink, the same pane of glass Tom had looked through earlier.

She ran her fingers along the edges of the new sink, breathed in the scent of freshly cut wood and a leftover hint of Tom's aftershave.

"So why did he need to talk to me?" Rose puzzled through the possibilities as she called in an order at the local Chinese bistro and donned her jacket to go get her dinner.

She still hadn't answered Fi, so she sat in the car while it idled and typed. *She is! She'll be twelve next month. You'll have to come out to Three Rivers and see her ride. It's incredible.*

She sent the message without acknowledging Ed's fiancée. What was she supposed to say anyway?

Rose pulled out of her driveway and drove, ignoring her phone when it buzzed. The Sheriff would be so proud that the loan manager wasn't texting and driving. Need consumed her, but she managed to keep her fingers firmly planted on the steering wheel all the way to Wok 'N Roll.

Fiona had sent a few messages.

I'll be there!

She seemed so much more engaged. And she remembered my name, and spoke to me. She hasn't done that for a while.

Rose smiled. She knew Mari would never be cured of her Autism, but she seemed to be functioning at a higher level since she began working with the doctors and horses at Courage Reins.

Her sister's last text set Rose's smile running for the hills.

The fiancée's name was Sierra. She was as tall as the day is long, and I've never seen hair so blonde.

Rose looked out her windshield, wondering what to say to Fiona. She seemed to want to talk about the fiancée, but Rose didn't know why she cared.

With her divorce final six years ago, Rose didn't concern herself with Ed's relationships beyond how a marriage and a step-mother would affect Mari. Understanding flooded her insides, eliminating her appetite, though Wok's made the best pork egg rolls within two hundred miles.

Ed wanted to talk to Rose because his upcoming marriage *would* affect Mari.

She immediately began to scramble for possibilities. Maybe Sierra was high-maintenance and didn't want Mari to come visit on weekends anymore.

Not fair, she chastised herself. *You don't even know the woman.*

She refused to allow herself to even come up with another maybe. She reached for her purse, her heart rate rocketing into the back of her throat when someone knocked on her window. She twisted to see who it was, her hands flying to her throat.

But it was only Chelsea, Pete's wife. She waved and straightened as she opened the car door. "That is you, Rose. I couldn't really tell with the glow from your phone."

Rose nabbed her purse and stood, closing the door behind her as she moved toward Chelsea. "Just texting my sister." She swallowed the lump in the back of her throat, the one bursting with words about her ex-husband and how he was moving to Hawaii with his new wife.

"You going to Wok's too?" Chelsea asked.

"Yeah, called in an order. Mari's in Amarillo with her dad."

Chelsea cast her a sideways glance. "I've told you to come out to the ranch when your daughter's gone." She held the door open for Rose, a friendly smile hitched in place.

Rose folded her arms and stopped in the doorway. "Why? So I can eat your Chinese take-out?" She laughed as she moved toward the pick-up counter, glad when Chelsea joined her. "Besides, you probably order the safe options here." She turned as she waited in line, satisfied at the mock horrified look on Chelsea's face.

"Safe options?" Chelsea glanced at the menu and tossed her dark ponytail over her shoulder. "What does that mean?"

Rose twisted and pointed to the sign. "See the ones with the little peppers to the side? Did you order any of those?"

Chelsea's lips scrunched into a distasteful smirk.

"I didn't think so," Rose said. "Let me guess. Sweet and sour chicken, and…beef with broccoli."

"Hey," Chelsea protested. "I'm still trying to lose the last twenty pounds of baby weight. Broccoli is healthy."

Rose giggled, beyond happy to have run into someone to distract her from her sister's texts. "How is your little munchkin? I didn't see her when I was out there last night."

Chelsea sighed, a pleased expression softening her features. "She's doin' just fine. She was asleep when you came. She's started teething and it wears her right out."

Rose nodded like she could remember Mari teething. But it had been too many years, and the tender moments of her daughter's childhood seemed held behind a film of discolored glass. So focused Rose stayed on the present, on helping Mari now, she didn't often pause to think of what she'd already accomplished.

The line inched forward, and Rose went with it, wondering if Ed would talk to Mari about his fiancée, or wait and have Rose do it. Anxiety increased Rose's pulse. She wanted to be there to help Mari understand.

"Rose?" Chelsea stepped in front of her, her blue eyes concerned.

Rose snapped herself back to the present. "Hmm? Sorry, I got lost."

"I asked if you wanted to come out to the ranch with me." She gestured toward the cash register, where only one person remained before it was their turn. "I'm sure Pete would love to see you, and

Garth's coming over too."

Rose almost asked if Tom would be there, but she bit down on the question. It took forty minutes to drive to the ranch. Did she want to go all that way just to eat?

"Yeah, sure," she said, knowing this was about more than eating. She needed to get out of her house—which was apparently more run down than she'd cared to acknowledge before Tom's visit.

The fact remained that Rose didn't have all that many people visit. Period. She was used to the way the house looked, and she didn't have time to paint walls and rip out carpet.

Tom didn't either.

Chelsea squealed and engulfed Rose in a hug. "I'm glad you're coming."

Rose couldn't erase the smile as she stepped up to the register and requested her order. She'd have her kung pow and spicy szechuan shrimp, and a healthy dose of adult conversation too.

Harry read back her order, and Rose realized how much she'd ordered. Heat rose to her cheeks as she handed over her debit card to pay. "I guess I ordered a little too much food."

"I call dibs on one of those pork rolls," Chelsea said, bumping Rose with her hip. "And it's okay. Maybe there'll be a couple other cowhands joining us." She waggled her phone like she'd just fired off half a dozen texts. She probably had.

Rose kept her attention on the waiter as he gathered her rather large paper sack. Harry handed back her card, which she tucked into her wallet before reaching for the food.

"Maybe I'll just go back to my place." Rose avoided looking at

Chelsea. She didn't want to hurt her feelings, but she didn't want to be paired off either. Even if she thought Tom was kind, gentle, and handsome—she'd only realized a new level of feelings for him that day. She didn't need Chelsea making things awkward between them.

"No, don't do that." Chelsea gave Harry her name. "I just thought...." She met Rose's eye, who stared at her with blazing determination.

"You just thought what?"

"I thought because you had so much food, you wouldn't mind if a couple more of the boys came over."

"Tom?" Rose challenged.

A guilty glint entered Chelsea's eyes, and now she was suddenly super interested in the waiter gathering her order. "Maybe Tom."

Rose groaned. "I don't need to be set up." She took a few steps away right as Chelsea's order arrived.

"Rose, wait."

Rose paused, her heartbeat thrumming against her breastbone. She had few friends, and she didn't want to alienate those she did have.

"I'm not trying to set you up."

"What are you trying to do?"

Chelsea blinked, clearly taken off-guard at the question. Rose stuffed away her bank manager exterior. Some called her intimidating, but she wasn't at work today, didn't need to verify every penny of income before approving a loan.

"It's okay, Chelsea." Rose attempted a smile, but it felt slightly sideways. "I'm really tired, and don't want to make the drive tonight. Another time though." She gave Chelsea a quick hug and headed for the door.

"Okay," Chelsea said, following her with her own bulky bags. "But I'm holding you to another time."

"Deal." Rose slid into her car and started the ignition. At least she tried to. Thankfully, Chelsea had already moved toward her luxury SUV, and Rose wondered how much the bank would need to lend her to be able to afford a car like that.

She clenched her jaw and tried the key again. A sputter, a rumble, and the engine came to life. Rose breathed in the smell of her spicy shrimp as she headed toward home. She couldn't afford a home improvement loan *and* a new car loan, and as she pulled into her driveway, where once again the automatic garage door wouldn't open, Rose knew which she preferred.

She ate her copious amount of Chinese food, in front of the TV, with little Paprika at her side. The dog didn't talk, but Rose didn't feel like conversing anyway. Even as a twinge of disappointment snagged in her chest that she might have missed Tom, she was supremely glad she hadn't gone out to Three Rivers tonight.

A knock sounded on Tom's door, and he almost ignored it. He could've made an excuse to anyone on the other side. Went out on the range. Stayed in town with his aunt. Anything.

But Winston whined, focused on the door and then swung his big Labrador head toward Tom. And whined again.

"I hear your dog," Pete called through the closed door.

"Traitor," Tom mumbled under his breath as he heaved himself off the couch. He'd ignored the Lieutenant's texts about coming over to the house for dinner. He didn't need more company after the several hours he'd spent with Rose. He'd already conversed more today than he usually did in a week.

Especially because he was sure news of his day trip into town to help the loan manager had made it through the gossip grapevine around Three Rivers. And that always ended with Chelsea trying to set something up.

He scratched Winston's head so the dog would know he wasn't really mad. He opened the door. "What's up, Pete?"

Tom had never told Pete that he'd also served in the Army, albeit briefly. He hadn't wanted to explain that he hadn't quite measured up. Tom stuffed those memories to the soles of his feet as he took in Pete's commanding form on his porch. Not measuring up seemed to be a recurring theme in Tom's life, one he'd finally started to break a couple years ago when Squire Ackerman, owner of Three Rivers Ranch, had made him the general controller.

He wasn't the foreman, but the controller paid better and provided better accommodations than cowhand.

"You eatin' by yourself?"

Biggest perk of being the controller: No roommate.

"Yeah."

"Chelsea wants you to come over to the house."

Tom forced a yawn through his lips. "Tell her thanks, but I'm beat."

Pete squinted at him, and Tom didn't like the way the man could see through a lie like it was made of plastic wrap.

"Where you been all day?"

"In town." The wind whipped through the alleyway in front of Tom's cabin. His sat next to Garth's, near the end of the row. But the administration trailer sat fifteen feet from his front porch, and the wind that came through the tunnel howled like a wolf.

"You wanna come in?" Tom asked as another blast of air came through.

Pete entered the cabin and bent down to pat Winston while Tom closed the door. "What's really going on?" he asked.

"Nothing." Pete straightened but wouldn't look at him.

"I already ate dinner." Tom scanned the cabin, though there wasn't a dirty dish in sight and he hadn't eaten.

"You're not a great liar." Pete smirked at him.

"Neither are you, Lieutenant." Tom folded his arms while Winston joined him at his side. At least the dog knew where his loyalty should be. "Did Chelsea invite a woman out to your place or something?"

Pete didn't even have to speak for Tom to know the answer. He rolled his eyes. "I'm doing just fine without you guys interfering." He reclaimed his spot on the couch and put his feet up on the coffee table he'd built with Brett last summer, right before Brett had been deployed for the fourth time.

Tom hadn't expressed the ache he held deep inside about wanting to be deployed. He'd never served overseas, but not for lack of trying. But he could never say as much to Brett, who viewed the deployment as the worst punishment he could've been given.

Tom hadn't blamed him. He'd already served overseas three times, and he'd just started to get to know the son he hadn't known he had. Tom missed Brett, but he didn't miss feeling like the odd man out, the fifth wheel, to Pete and Chelsea, and Brett and Kate.

They lived in North Carolina now, and last Tom had heard, Brett had made it home to his wife and son in one piece.

"I heard you went to Rose's today."

"Heard from who?" Tom slid Pete a wary glance, glad when the man didn't join him on the couch.

"Ethan."

"I'm going to have to choose a less mouthy cowhand to cover my chores next time."

Pete settled on the edge of the table. "So there *will* be a next time."

Tom shot to his feet. "I'm goin' to bed. You know how to lock the door on your way out?" He strode away from Pete's low chuckle and Winston's high whine, heat blazing in his face. He never should've said anything to anyone about going into town to help Rose. He could've made up a story about visiting his aunt, or driving to Amarillo for the day.

Then he could suffer in his own idiocy without having everyone—human and animal alike—know about his inadequacy when it came to women.

The next morning, Tom leaned against his front porch railing while he waited for Garth to emerge from his cabin. He whistled the tune his daddy used to while they were setting fences or feeding chickens, about the only two things he'd let Tom help with before age twelve.

After that, Tom learned the ins and outs of ranching, from branding the cattle to hauling hay to birthing calves. Tom had done it all, and loved it. He'd spoken true when he'd told Rose as much.

But there had been a few years where he'd set his sights on something else. Someone else. Tried to be someone different from who he was. He glanced into the sky, which cast a gray light down on him.

Who am I, Lord? he thought. His only answer came in another gust of spring air and the banging of Garth's door as he opened it and the wind caught it.

Tom wasn't entirely sure he wanted to spend the rest of his life in a three-room cabin on a ranch in Texas, even if he had the place to himself. He'd always felt there was something more for him, but he didn't know what.

"Mornin'," Garth said as he secured his door. "Am I driving?"

"I can, if you want." Tom snapped his fingers at Winston, who stood and strolled down the steps to meet him. "I told my aunt I'd come for lunch after church. If you don't want—"

"That's fine," Garth said, maybe a little too fast.

Tom glanced at him, trying to get a read on the man without staring. Garth seemed as cool as ever, his hands tucked into his slacks and his blue eyes steady.

"She's makin' barbeque," Tom added.

"Even better." Garth grinned.

"I took care of all the mandatory chores." Tom stepped toward the path that led to the parking lot, Garth behind him and Winston beside him. "Ethan said he'd do the afternoon feedings."

Garth grunted his approval as Tom climbed into the driver's seat of his truck. He'd been going to church with Garth since the foreman's arrival a couple years ago, and the silence between them felt normal. Almost comforting.

So Tom's nerves leapt particularly high when Garth said, "Can I ask you a question?"

Tom tightened his grip on the steering wheel. "Sure, boss."

"How old do you think I am?"

Tom could drive the road from the ranch to town with his eyes closed, so he focused on Garth for a few seconds. "I don't know. Forty?"

"Forty?" Garth snarled and removed his cowboy hat so he could run his fingers through his hair.

"Too old?" Tom asked, giving his attention to the road.

"About a decade too old."

"How old do you think I am?"

"I know how old you are," he said. "I authorize your check every two weeks, Mister Not a Day Over Twenty-Seven."

Tom shrugged. "Sorry?" He snuck another glance at Garth. "Why are you askin'?"

Garth stuffed his hat back on his head, effectively hiding his salt and pepper hair. "No reason."

Tom chuckled. "Okay, boss. But you should know everyone finds out everything on the ranch."

"Yeah, like you havin' your eye on that Rose Reyes."

Exhaustion descended on Tom as he sighed. "I don't have my eye on her. We're *friends*. She needed help with her kitchen sink is all." He lifted one shoulder like the conversation topic didn't make his stomach boil with nerves—or anticipation for when he could see Rose again.

"She ask you to come help with her sink?"

"Yeah." Tom cast Garth a look that asked what that had to do with anything.

"Maybe she wants to be more than friends."

Tom couldn't help thinking about the way she'd gazed at him while they both knelt on her kitchen floor. The spark had been as hot as anything Tom had felt with a woman. He kept his body rigid as he struggled for an answer.

"She...has a daughter." He pressed a bit harder on the accelerator, ready to get to church so this conversation could end. "With special needs. She just needs a friend to help with a few...." He trailed off as he remembered the wonder in her eyes, the heat in her face when he'd asked for his hat. The way she wouldn't make eye contact with him once she'd handed it over. "Home renovations."

"If you haven't asked, then she might be interested in more than kitchen sinks." Garth's false tone held dozens of implications, none of which Tom particularly liked.

"I don't see you datin' anyone," Tom said. "I thought it was because you were nearing retirement, but—"

Garth's boisterous laugh drowned out Tom's next words, and he couldn't help laughing too.

They quieted just as Tom pulled into the church parking lot. The way the trees bent over, the wind here was obviously just as brutal as out on the range.

"I don't really think you're nearing retirement." Tom glanced at Garth's hat. "But you have some gray hair. Can't blame me for thinking you were older."

Garth waved away his words. "It's no big deal. It's just I may have my eye on someone myself." He unbuckled his seat belt and slid from the truck before Tom could comprehend his words.

By the time his mind caught up, Garth had covered half the distance to the door. Tom scrambled after him, battling against the wind.

"Who?" he practically shouted as they reached the door.

Garth glared at him. "Later," he ground out between clenched teeth.

"Who?" Tom ducked through the door into the quieter lobby. Relief flowed through him to be out of the wind, that it was the Sabbath and he didn't have to go out into the oncoming storm to do chores.

"Juliette." Garth smiled over Tom's shoulder and stepped past him without a backward glance. Tom turned and watched as his aunt and his boss exchanged hellos and entered the chapel ahead of him.

He stared, not quite believing. His aunt and Garth? *Juliette* and

Garth? How had Tom missed that?

They sat by Juliette every week at church, had gone to her place for lunch several times. Tom had never noticed anything romantic blooming between them. *A lot like me and Rose,* he thought. He'd never truly *seen* her, despite people teasing him about her. As if summoned by his thoughts, Rose entered the building, bringing the wind with her.

"Hey," he said, seizing the distraction.

"Morning." Rose grinned at him. "You're not alone, are you?" She peered behind him, though most of the churchgoers had already gone into the chapel.

"No, I'm—" He hooked his thumb over his shoulder and stopped talking. "I mean, yeah. Do you need someone to sit by?"

Rose ducked her chin and unzipped her jacket. "Mari is gone until this evening, so I'd love a pew partner." She began to shrug out of her coat, but it snagged on her shoulder. Tom reached out to help her, sliding the fabric down her arm and over her elbow until it released.

Heat sprang from her to him, and every cell in his body fired on all cylinders. His muscles tensed, ready for fight or flight. His eyes caught hers, and he didn't have to ask Rose if she'd go out with him to know she was interested. He saw it burning in the depths of her gorgeous eyes.

He couldn't help the grin as it curved his mouth. He offered her his elbow. "Shall we?"

Chapter Four

The nearness of Tom kept Rose on edge through the whole service. She was used to getting nothing from the sermons, as she usually devoted all her energy to keeping Mari entertained and quiet. But today she couldn't focus to save her life.

Tom sat casually, with his hands hanging between his knees, his attention on the pulpit singular.

She stared unabashedly at him as he seemed so focused on what Pastor Scott was saying. Rose hadn't heard a single word. The buzz from Tom's touch hummed in her ears, warmed her stomach, warned her of getting too close to him.

He sat a good eight inches away—definitely not too close. *Definitely not close enough.*

Rose startled at her thoughts and slipped another inch between them.

"Are you gonna stare at me the whole time?" Tom leaned his whole body toward hers and barely moved his lips as he whispered.

Rose's body felt consumed with flames. She jerked her eyes from his chiseled jaw, surprised she'd been so focused on it.

"I suppose I don't mind." He shifted closer to her, the hint of his aftershave tickling her senses. She basked in the woodsy quality of it, the fresh pine, the spicy sandalwood.

He lifted his arm and settled it on the back of the pew behind her, his hand dangling lazily near her arm. "Can I ask you something?" He kept his gaze on the pulpit, never once glancing at her.

She could only nod, something he seemed to be able to see though he wouldn't look.

"My aunt Juliette is makin' her famous Texas barbeque after church. Garth and I are going. You want to come?"

Rose's thoughts scattered, leaving only one behind: Was he asking her out on a date? Or simply to a friendly lunch at his aunt's house because he knew Rose had an empty house to go home to?

With the thought of Mari, Rose's defenses flew back into place. Her automatic reaction was to say no. But Mari wasn't here....

"Sure," she whispered, crossing her legs so she leaned closer to him. "I just have to be back to my place about five for Mari."

"No problem." Tom finally turned toward her, lowering his head so his mouth hovered just above her ear. "Next week, you get to sit on this side so I can stare at you." He chuckled, barely making a sound at all, but Rose felt the reverberations clear down in her soul.

Rose followed Tom's ranch truck past the elementary school, the park, the grocer, and into the newer part of town on the northwest side. The houses sat in neat rows, nearly identical in cut and color. The lawns had started greening, the trees were flowering.

Rose envied the tidiness of it all. Everything in her life felt overgrown and sideways, especially since she didn't know what to do with her growing feelings for Tom. Her heart warred with her mind, each one casting reasons for why a relationship with him would work, and why it wouldn't.

She arrived at the end of the street, at a house with a blue door, as confused as ever. She parked, the engine of her car idling hard enough for her to feel under the brake pedal. She twisted the key out of the ignition, half hoping this fierce wind would steal away her car so she could get a new one.

Tom waited at the door of his truck while she came up the drive. He kicked a friendly grin in her direction, and she wished it didn't jumpstart her pulse to pounding. Or maybe she wanted it to. She wasn't sure.

What she was sure about was that she didn't want to risk her friendship with Tom. Didn't want to upset or change more in Mari's life. But something nagged at her that she deserved happiness too. She should be able to date and find someone worth marrying, the way Ed had. Why did he get to and she didn't?

"You like barbeque?" Tom asked as they headed up the front sidewalk together. Tom's boss, Garth, had already stepped through the front door.

"What Texas girl doesn't?" Rose flashed Tom a quick smile. "My daddy used to make the best brisket in five counties." A sudden pang of homesickness hit her. Her parents lived a few hundred miles south, and with her full-time job she didn't get down to

Dallas to see them as often as she'd like.

Her father ran a non-profit organization that helped put food on the table for those who didn't have it. And he was the best cook Rose knew. Her mouth watered for some of her father's cornbread and whipped raspberry butter.

"Where are your parents living?" Tom asked.

"They're still in Dallas," Rose said. "What about yours?"

Tom stilled with his hand on the doorknob. "Dad's in Montana. Mom's…I don't know where my mother currently is." A hard edge rode in his tone, and Rose's curiosity rose a notch.

"Siblings?" she asked, hoping that subject wasn't taboo.

"One brother. Older. Jace works the ranch with my dad." He turned the knob and pushed the door in. "Aunt Juliette?" He nodded into the house. "Juliette is my father's youngest sister. She's a bit—" He couldn't finish the sentence before a dog the size of a small horse barreled toward them.

Rose yelped and stepped behind Tom as a tall, thin woman followed the dog. A grin split her face and she pulled Tom and Rose into the house with a squeal and a laugh. "Get in here, honey. I have your sweet tea as cold as a polar bear in an igloo."

Juliette released Tom and sized up Rose in two heartbeats. "Hey, honey, it's real nice to meet you." She glanced at Tom, her meaning clear.

"Aunt Juliette, this is my friend, Rose Reyes. Her daughter comes riding out at the ranch."

Rose's heart shriveled a little at the introduction, though she wasn't sure why. She *was* Tom's friend. Her daughter did ride out at the ranch. Him squeezing her fingers for one second over coffee didn't make a relationship. But maybe snuggling together in a pew at church did.

That wasn't snuggling, she reminded herself. They hadn't even been touching.

"Nice to meet you, ma'am," Rose said, taking some of the warmth from Juliette's voice and infusing it into hers.

"Oh, honey, don't ma'am me. That's for women twice my age." She tucked her elbow into Tom's. "Now come get your sweet tea." She led him into the airy kitchen, where Garth sat at a long bar sipping tea from a tall glass.

Rose admired the open layout of the house, how she could see from the front door all the way to the backyard. She wondered if Tom was handy enough to remodel her entire floor to make it more like this.

Knowing him and his capable hands, Rose suspected the answer was yes. Heat licked her face as she tried to contain her fantasies. Tom had barely grazed her shoulder with his hands, and she had no idea how capable they were.

She took the sweet tea and sipped it, the sugar exploding on her tongue. She moaned without meaning to.

"See?" Juliette laughed in Tom's direction. "I *am* the best sweet tea brewer in the South."

Tom gulped his tea. "The very best." He glanced at Rose. "My aunt really is a great cook."

"Oh, go on." Juliette waved an oven mitt before slipping her delicate hand into it and stepping onto the back porch. She lifted the lid on a charcoal grill, the smoke immediately being whisked to the right.

She worked the tongs in quick, short strokes, and returned a minute later. "Almost done." She huffed and removed the oven mitt. "So, Rose, tell me about yourself."

Rose's muscles bunched and released, all within half a second. "I work at the bank. I'm the loan manager."

"Where are you from?"

"Dallas."

"Been married before?"

"Aunt Juliette," Tom warned, sliding a pleading look to Garth.

Garth stood from his barstool. "Juliette, can I talk to you for a second?" He opened the sliding glass door and stepped into the wind. Juliette cast Tom an apologetic look before joining Garth outside.

"Sorry," Tom said once the door had slid into place. "She's eccentric, as I was trying to say before we got mobbed by Betsy Ross."

Rose took a gulp of her sweet tea. "The dog's name is Betsy Ross?"

Tom shrugged. "Juliette's patriotic. Loves her dogs. She's a veterinarian technician."

Rose giggled. "I like her."

Tom smiled, but he kept his gaze glued out the door, where Garth and Juliette stood. She moved to his side and followed his watchful eye. "They're cute."

"Yeah," Tom ground out. "Cute." He turned away and visibly

relaxed. He collapsed into a chair facing away from the porch and lifted his hat to scrub one hand through his hair. Rose wondered what his hair felt like, if the stubble along his jaw would scratch, if she could somehow help him reassure him of his worth the way he'd done for her.

She sank into the chair near his and enjoyed a moment of peace. All too soon, Mari returned to her mind, crowding in with Ed and what he needed to speak with her about.

The sound of the door opening interrupted her thoughts. The scent of perfectly smoked meat came with it, and Rose stood to offer Juliette help. She stirred baked beans in a crock pot and placed napkins on the table, grateful she was here this afternoon instead of at home alone.

As they joined hands and said grace, Rose realized how much she'd been missing by not having family nearby. A zing sped up her arm when Tom kept her fingers in his for an extra beat, and for one brief moment, she saw the exact hole he filled in her life.

Fear and hope blipped through her with every beat of her heart.

Fear, fear...hope.

Hope, hope...fear.

Her body couldn't make up its mind as to which emotion she felt stronger.

"Aunt Juliette, I can't possibly eat all that." Tom watched as she continued to ladle baked beans into a plastic container.

"I can," Garth said from his place at the table. The Texas

weather usually allowed them to eat on Juliette's back deck, but the wind hadn't relented all afternoon, and they'd stayed indoors.

"Only heaven knows what you can eat," Juliette said over her shoulder, a flirtatious tone in her voice and a grin on her face. Tom had endured similar exchanges for hours. So many hours he wondered how he'd missed the sparks between his boss and his aunt before today. He and Garth had eaten at Juliette's lots of times, and never once had Tom suspected anything.

Garth's obvious flirting had left Tom with a queasy feeling in his stomach. He hadn't flirted with a woman in a while, and didn't even know how to start with Rose. She hadn't seemed to mind the company, the food, or the questions his aunt asked.

Juliette was in her mid-thirties, the youngest sister of Tom's dad, and she had one divorce in her past. Tom wanted her to find someone to share her life with. He'd just never expected it to be someone he knew so well.

He found himself staring at Garth—again. He pulled his eyes away as Juliette started filling another container of beans. "You want some, honey?" She'd been calling everyone honey for as long as Tom could remember.

Rose took it in stride, and though she didn't seem like the huggy type, she'd folded right into his aunt's embrace when they'd arrived. Tom had been thinking about doing that to Rose too. In fact, he couldn't seem to focus on much else.

But spending the afternoon with Rose nearby had soothed him, the same way it had yesterday. He checked the time again, the minutes ticking closer to when Rose needed to leave. She caught him looking and raised her eyebrows.

"I should probably get going," she said. "Walk me out, Tom?"

He practically leapt from the table. "Comin'." He didn't look back as he exited the kitchen a couple of steps behind Rose. "You don't have to go quite yet," he said as she reached the front door.

"I don't want to be late."

He helped her into her coat. "Do I have time to come have a cup of coffee?" He didn't want to let her go quite yet, and he didn't think Garth would complain if he could spend some alone time with Juliette.

"Depends on how fast you can drink." She flashed him a smile as she fished her car keys out of her jacket pocket.

"Didn't you say Ed wanted to talk to you?" he asked. "I can entertain Mari while you talk." Tom fell back a step like he didn't care, but a next of snakes writhed in his stomach.

"All right. Let's go, cowboy." She twisted the doorknob and stepped into the still howling wind.

Tom spun back to the kitchen and moved back to the doorway. "I'll be back in a little bit, okay?"

Garth grinned and tipped his hat, paving the way for Tom to leave. He drove the few miles to Rose's in silence, his thumbs drumming against the steering wheel, those snakes coiling and striking.

"It's just coffee," he muttered to himself, pushing his hat lower over his eyes. He knew it wasn't just coffee. Rose knew it too.

Tom pulled into her driveway, unsure of the next step. Did he ask her out? Could he hug her tonight? He hadn't been in this position in a very long time, if ever. Desi had been much more forward, more flirty, more in control.

He took a cleansing breath and walked to the front door. He knocked at the same time Rose opened the door. "Coffee's on. Come on in."

Tom entered her house, grateful for the blast of heat. "Thanks." They moved into the kitchen, where Tom examined the cabinets she obviously hadn't touched since he'd left yesterday. "I can stain these—"

"I'll get to it." The frost in her tone suggested he drop the subject.

He didn't want to, but something nagged the back of his mind. "All right, *honey*." His aunt's words flowed from his mouth easily, and he added her extra-strong twang.

Rose stiffened at the same time Tom broke into laughter. "Yeah, that doesn't really work for us, does it?" He closed the distance between them and took the empty mug she held in her hand. He poured a cup of coffee and handed it to her.

She took a sip, her eyes holding his above the rim of her mug. "Us?"

"You always have cream and sugar," he said, sidestepping her question. His mind blanked as he poured another cup of coffee for himself. His brain literally sent no signals to the rest of his body, but he'd drank enough coffee to operate on muscle memory for the time being.

"I—" A knock on the door saved Tom from stuttering through a lame response about his attempt at flirting.

Rose startled and set her mug on the counter before hurrying through the door and into the living room. Tom exhaled heavily and stepped to the window. The backyard needed so much work, it made his fingers twitch to get out there and start weeding. If it meant he could spend time with Rose, he'd do just about anything.

Surprised by the intensity of his feelings for a woman he knew only superficially, Tom tried to swallow them away. They wouldn't go.

Voices floated to his ears from the other room, and Tom moved to the doorway and leaned into it. He sized up Rose's ex-husband, a tall man with broad shoulders, dark hair, and even darker eyes.

Tom wouldn't acknowledge the similarities between himself and her ex, though they were plain for anyone to see.

They spoke in low tones, and Tom took a few quiet steps to where Mari stood. "Hey, Mari," he whispered. "Want to come show me your dog?"

"Tom," she said. "Paprika."

He smiled at her. "Right. Paprika. Where is she?"

"She's in my bedroom, baby," Rose said. "Go get her and take her out, okay?"

Mari turned and moved down the hallway, but Tom didn't follow her. He eased back into the kitchen so he wouldn't have to face Rose's ex-husband. Thankfully, Mari only took a few seconds to return with a black and white dog tucked under one arm. She continued through the kitchen and dining room—which needed new windows if the draft Tom felt was any indication—and into the garage.

He followed her all the way into the backyard, where she set down the dog. "Go on," she told Paprika, and the little dog ran into the jungle that Rose called a backyard.

"How was your visit with your dad?" Tom asked.

Mari crouched down at the edge of the patio and drew her finger through a patch of dirt.

Tom appreciated her presence, her gentle soul, the silence between them that didn't feel strained. He knelt next to her and added his lines to her drawing. She wouldn't look at him, but he was used to that. He was used to giving her instructions and asking her questions and having her remain quiet.

"Too long," she said, smudging out part of a curve he'd drawn.

"What are you drawing?"

"Paprika." She pointed to the yard-jungle without looking up, though the dog was nowhere to be seen.

Several seconds later, Tom saw the lines come together to form a very realistic version of Mari's dog.

"Look at that," he said. "It's great, Mari."

She beamed at him, stood, and spanked the dirt from her hands. "Paprika!" she called, and the little dog came running through the undergrowth.

"Hey, baby." Rose appeared, sliding her arm around Mari's shoulders. "Did you have fun at Dad's?"

Mari scooped up the dog and turned toward the house. "Yeah, fun."

Rose rubbed her hands together. "Thanks, Tom."

"Sure thing, ma'am."

She half-laughed, half-sobbed as she swatted at him. "If you start calling me ma'am, I'll start blocking your calls."

Tom laughed with her, catching her wrist as she came at him again. "Aw, come on. You can't do that."

She sobered and stilled as he slid his fingers between hers. "What did Ed have to say?" He saw the turmoil in her eyes, the near-tears threatening to spill over. He guided her closer, tucked her close against his side as if he could protect her that way.

She sniffled. "He's getting married, and apparently, his company is opening a new branch in Washington. He's up for the position."

The bitterness in her voice made him cringe. "I'm sorry, Rose."

She shrugged. "He hasn't gotten the job yet, but he says there will be a lot of travel this summer, and he might not be able to take Mari as often as he usually does." She ducked her head, tucking herself into his chest. He encircled her in his arms, a thrill shooting from his boots to his brain when she hugged him back.

Tom could barely think through the haze fogging his mind. "I'll take her whenever you need a break," he managed to say.

Rose scoffed and let her arms fall from his back. Tom missed her touch so much a sharp ache cut through his core.

"Right. You'll take my daughter." She paced away from him.

"I will. She loves the ranch. She can come out there and work with the horses." He shoved his hands in his pockets. "You have to let people help you, Rose."

She spun back to him, a fire sparking in her eyes. "I let people help me."

Tom chuckled, but it was tinged with sarcasm. "Sure you do.

Like you let me help you with your house."

A muscle in Rose's jaw jumped jumped jumped. Tom wished he didn't find her frustration so attractive. He almost smiled, but smothered it just in time.

"Fine, you can come help me with the house."

"Really?" Tom cocked his eyebrows.

"It's better than babysitting my daughter," she growled as she strode back into the garage.

"I'll do both," Tom called after her, totally pressing his luck. He joined her in the house. "Really, Rose, it's—"

"Tom," she said, sending him a glare from where she stood in the kitchen, helping Mari butter toast. "We'll see you next weekend, okay?"

Tom's heart beat out a dance of happiness. He tipped his hat. "Sounds good, *ma'am*." He chuckled and ducked through the door as Rose cried out in protest.

Chapter Five

Relief weighed on Rose when she entered the bank the next morning. She'd suffered through a long night, first with talking to Mari about the upcoming changes in her life. Mari hadn't seemed too upset, and Rose wondered if Ed had spoken with her already. The better explanation, and the one that had kept Rose awake long into the night, was that Mari didn't fully understand the forthcoming changes.

One thing Rose knew: Mari didn't deal that well with change of any kind. She'd stared at the new cabinet in the kitchen that didn't match the others, ran her fingers along the new sink like it might suddenly coil into a rattlesnake and strike.

So dropping her off at the academy and entering her office became a balm to Rose's weary soul. She kept the door closed as she turned on her computer and reviewed the files she hadn't been able to finish last week.

Before beginning, though, she pulled out a blank loan application and picked up a pen. If Tom was going to come over and help spruce up the house, Rose needed some money to pay for it.

She also needed a transplant of willpower, because just being in the same room with Tom seemed to make her good sense flee. New to the flirting game after many years in hibernation, Rose wasn't sure exactly what was happening between them. She knew she liked being with Tom, more than usual. She appreciated his steadiness, his willingness to help, the slightly dangerous glint in his eye when he held her hand.

Her fingers tingled as she signed her name. She couldn't approve her own loan application, so she walked the forms over to Jason Budge, the bank's manager.

"I need a home improvement loan," she said as she sank into a chair opposite his desk.

He glanced up at her. "Oh, good morning, Rose." He took the papers she slid across the desk to him. "A home improvement loan?"

"Yeah, my house needs a little remodeling. I have a friend coming to help me. This is just for supplies." Her traitorous tongue tripped over the word *friend*.

Jason scanned the document. "Sounds good. I know you'll make the payment." He scribbled his approval in the boxes at the bottom of the form, the same place Rose usually made her administrative notes.

With the signed papers in her hands, Rose retreated back to her office. She gripped the application in tight fingers, a slow smile spreading across her face. She was really doing this. Really committing to fixing up her house. Really committing to spending many weekends in the future with Tom.

Giddiness pranced through her, a sensation Rose allowed herself to enjoy for several seconds. Then she pulled out her cell phone and sent Tom a text.

Just got the financial approval for our home improvement projects. Can we meet before Saturday to discuss what I'll need to buy?

Tom didn't answer right away, not that she expected him to. She knew he ran a tight ship with the cowhands, and that included no cell phones while on the job. She remembered him disciplining a cowboy for texting when he should've been hauling hay.

She'd seen his downturned mouth, the regret in his eyes. Tom didn't like inflicting punishments, but he took managing the cowhands very seriously.

Rose tucked her phone and the approved paperwork into her purse, a sigh leaving her body. Like she needed another reason to admire Tom, though it seemed his gentle demeanor was definitely going in the plus column.

Rose double-checked to ensure the folder she'd prepared still sat in her purse. Of course it did. It was there when she left for work. There when she checked mid-morning. There when she'd left for the diner. There at the last red light she'd stopped at.

Still there.

She took a deep breath and pushed into the diner, a local joint that had been in Three Rivers since the town's inception. Remodels, new owners, and updated menu items kept the residents happy and coming back for more.

Tom sitting in a corner booth made Rose smile, something she quickly stuffed away as she clicked her way toward him.

He raised his head and saw her, his midnight eyes brightening as he stood. "Afternoon, Rose."

"Hey, cowboy." She let him help her with her jacket before she slid into the booth opposite of him. She kept her purse tucked tight against her side, the nerves in her stomach blossoming into small tidal waves of apprehension.

"Coffee?" The waitress held two pots of brew, decaf and regular.

"Yes, regular," Rose said, sliding her mug closer to the edge of the table.

She filled the mug. "Y'all let me know when you're ready to order." She strode behind the counter and replaced the pots on their warmers before picking up an order.

Rose poured cream and sugar in her coffee, her mind rebelling against her. Why was talking to Tom suddenly so hard? Only days ago, she'd borne her darkest confession to him. Shared lunch with him. Held his hand and cried into his chest.

"So—" she began at the same time Tom said, "I think I'll get the bacon cheeseburger."

His announcement made her insides relax. "I like the tostada," she said. "With ranch dressing. Ranch is Mari's favorite."

She cringed inwardly, not sure why she'd brought up Mari. Perhaps as a way to remind herself to be professional about this lunch. This wasn't a date. It was a meeting. Him coming to help her with the house wasn't anything more than a professional arrangement. She had paperwork and everything.

She'd spent the last two days making pact after pact with herself, usually in the dead of night when she couldn't sleep.

Learn from him; let him teach you. But don't get too close.

Don't get attached to him.

Don't let your guard down in weak moments. No more crying. No more hugging. No more of any of that. Professionalism.

She pulled the folder from her purse. "Here is a list of things I think need to be done to the house. I've listed them with my priorities at the top."

Tom took the sheet of paper she extended toward him, but his eyes never left hers. When they finally did to roam down the list, he let out a low whistle.

"You've calculated it to the penny." This time when he looked at her, amusement danced through his expression.

"I am a loan manager," she said. "And I have to pay that money back, so I don't want any to go to waste."

He set the paper aside. "Of course not." He flagged down the waitress, who came over. He ordered for both of them and placed his hands on the table.

"A new garage door is priority number one," he said. "Well, we won't do that first, but I know a guy out of Amarillo. He can hook us up with a good deal."

Relief soared through Rose. "That sounds great."

"I'll call him this afternoon."

"So what do I need to buy before Saturday?"

Tom glanced up as the waitress arrived with their food. He sat back in the booth and waited while she set down his cheeseburger and fries and Rose's tostada. He thanked her and took a bite of his French fries.

Rose poured ranch dressing on her salad. "So what should I go get? I'll have the money by this afternoon."

He glanced at the list, still sitting on his side of the table. He cleared his throat and ate another French fry.

"Tom?"

"Let's stay in the kitchen. We can rip out the floor and lay down a nice engineered hardwood. Paint the walls something light. Maybe blue or gray. Replace the baseboards, the light fixtures, the countertops."

Rose's stomach warred against the single bite of lettuce she'd eaten. The more he spoke, the less sense he made.

"Can I do all that with the twenty thousand I've budgeted?"

"Yeah, sure," he said. "And more. We'll put in new carpet in the living room and take a look at your bathroom. You've got cheap labor." He gave her a grin that made it impossible to swallow. She tried anyway, and ended up coughing. She reached for her water glass, heat licking into her face. She finally managed to quiet down, but her thoughts continued to race around the idea of Tom working in her small kitchen.

"We can probably even replace your appliances with stainless steel," he said. "Let's do a little shopping on Friday night."

Rose's throat closed again, but this time she didn't try to swallow. "Both of us?"

"Sure," Tom said. "Do you have a design aesthetic in mind?"

Rose gulped her water, trying to get the heat in her cheeks to dissipate. She put down her fork and looked Tom square in the eyes. "Look, I'm going to be honest. I have no idea what I'm doing. I don't know what a design aesthetic is." She moaned. "I'm way in over my head here, aren't I?"

Tom chuckled, reached over, and covered one of her hands with his. A pulse shot from the warmth of his skin into hers, skittering all the way up her arm. "Totally in too deep," he said. "But I know a countertop guy, too, and I can get this kitchen done for way less than twenty grand."

He pulled his hand back and picked up his burger, seemingly unfazed. Rose still couldn't get her arm to retract from its spot on the table. Her skin felt cold, clammy.

He nodded to the folder. "What else you got in there?"

Rose took a deep breath and pushed her tostada out of the way. "I totally trust you, Tom, but this is a work agreement." She extracted a piece of paper and handed it to him. "It says you're going to do work we agree upon and I'm going to pay for supplies." She cleared her throat, wishing he didn't look so delicious in his cowboy hat. "I have also budgeted to pay you a small stipend from the loan."

He started shaking his head before she finished speaking. "Nope, not gonna take your money, Rose."

"It's not much. Don't get excited."

"How much?" He glanced up from the contract he held.

She leaned up and peered over the top of the paper, scanning to find the line. "Right there." She jabbed at the paper with her finger.

"Five thousand dollars?" Tom tossed the paper on top of her priority list, a disgusted look on his face. "I am not taking anything." He sat back in the booth and glared at her with those intense eyes.

Rose lost herself in their depths for a moment, before reminding herself of her personal pacts. "You are, Tom, or I'll find someone else to play weekend handyman."

Horror crossed his face, and a ruddy blush colored his neck as he leaned toward her as if they were having a hushed conversation they didn't want anyone to overhear. "It's too much. I don't need your money."

Some of the fight left Rose's body, and she leaned into the table too. "I know you don't, but I want to give it to you. I don't know what you'll have to do out on the ranch to be able to leave and come help me. But I don't want—I *will not*—be a burden to you."

"Rose—" He looked away helplessly, as if at a loss for words.

Rose straightened, fixing on her professional mask. "So do we have a deal, cowboy?" She pulled a pen from her purse. "You sign right there, and I'm all yours on Friday night."

Tom's gaze flew to hers. "All mine?"

Rose realized her flub as she took in the interest in his eyes, the air between them charged with something Rose had only felt a handful of times in her life. "All yours," she repeated, feeling daring and wild and very un-Rose-like.

He fumbled for the pen and whipped his signature on the page. "I'll pick you up about six. Does that work?"

Rose nodded as he handed back her paperwork. "I'll have Mari with me. She loves the hardware store because she can get as much popcorn as she wants, so she shouldn't be a problem."

Tom chuckled and reached for his burger. "A girl after my own heart."

Rose finally managed to force down a few bites of her lunch, but Tom's heated look, the strain in his voice when he asked "All mine?" circled in her mind for the rest of the day.

Tom arrived at Rose's at five minutes to six and hopped from the cab of his truck with a spring in his step. He'd asked Kenny, a quiet cowhand, to cover the evening chores with the promise of a gallon of mint chocolate chip ice cream from Patty's Parlor.

Nerves knotted his stomach but couldn't erase the euphoria that he'd been floating on for the past two days. Since meeting Rose for lunch on Wednesday, he hadn't been able to get her out of his mind. He wasn't sure if such constant thoughts were normal. He'd never felt this strongly about a woman before, not even Desi.

He knocked on the door and stuffed his hands in his jacket pockets. Minutes passed and no one answered the door. Tom swallowed back the urge to beat down the door with both fists. Instead, he rang the doorbell.

Light shone through a crack in the curtains. Rose's car sat in the driveway. She had to be here.

A moment later, the door swung open. Mari stood there, blinking at him with bloodshot eyes.

"Mari." He knelt in front of her. "What's wrong, honey?" He

glanced over the girl's shoulder and found Rose loitering in the kitchen doorway, her arms folded and her eyes sparking with frustration.

"Come in," Mari said, standing back and letting Tom enter the living room. She sent Rose the vilest glare Tom had seen Mari give, and he couldn't help chuckling. Thankfully, the low noise seemed to shatter the tension in the air.

"Are you girls ready for an epic trip to the hardware store?"

"Popcorn," Mari said.

"Yes," Tom said, reaching for Mari's hand. "There will be a lot of popcorn. But you can't scarf it down. We'll be there a while." With his free hand, he produced a list from his back pocket. "We have a lot of things to get."

He moved through the living room to where Rose still stood. He wanted to take her hand too, but schooled the urge. "Are you going to eat a lot of popcorn?"

She gazed up at him, and if Mari were at Ed's this weekend, and Tom was here alone on a Friday night, he could imagine kissing Rose, making hot chocolate in her newly remodeled kitchen, and tucking himself under a blanket with her while they watched a movie together.

The fantasy played out in his mind in full color as she looked at him.

"Tom," Mari said. "Let's go." She tugged on his hand, and he went with her. He reached his free hand back to Rose, beckoning her to come with them.

She smiled, shook her head, and shouldered her purse. He had

Mari loaded in the truck by the time Rose came out of the house, and he took a second to walk around to the passenger side with her. He put his hand on the door handle before she could, and leaned down so his mouth was level with her ear.

"You look great," he whispered. "Rough night?"

She lifted one hand to his forearm, her eyes pressed closed for a moment while she took a deep drag of air. "Just a small argument over who got to answer the door. Mari's not particularly good at it." Rose removed her hand and fell back a step. "She was angry with me for saying so."

Tom frowned, at both her words and her distance. "I thought she did great."

"She did." Rose smiled. "The best she's ever done." Something flittered through her expression, moving so fast Tom couldn't catch it. She leaned into him again, tilting her chin back to look at him. Inches separated his mouth from hers, and Tom's heart vaulted into a drumming rhythm.

"There's something about you, cowboy. Something as magical as Peony when it comes to Mari."

Tom felt his whole face break into a grin when Rose called him cowboy. She'd done it a few times at the diner too, but this time he heard adoration in the two syllables. Adoration for him.

"Ah, shucks, ma'am," he said, shuffling his feet so he was closer to her. "Just doin' the best I can."

Rose found his fingers with hers and squeezed. "Well, keep doing it. Minus the *ma'am* part." She released his hand in favor of the door handle and opened the passenger door to climb in beside her daughter.

"Tom," Mari said. "Hurry."

"I'm coming," he told her. "Hold your horses."

Tom got up a half hour early on Saturday morning in order to get the chores done in the barn before he headed over to Rose's. He was also expecting Jace to call with an update on their father, and he didn't want to miss it.

He paused outside Houdini's stall and waited for the horse to come over. Tom ran his fingers through the horse's hair, and all the pent-up worries and tension seeped out of his muscles.

"When the weather finally turns, we'll head out to the cabin," he promised the horse. "There'll be cows to round up, you know."

Houdini snuffled at Tom as if to say, *Duh, I round up cows every spring.*

The annual round-up was a few weeks away, and Tom had already told Rose he wouldn't be able to work on her kitchen that weekend.

"Goin' to Rose's today," he told Houdini. Peony's ears perked up at the mention of Rose, but the mare didn't stray over to the fence between the two stalls. "We're going to paint walls and stain cabinets and probably rip out some old tile. Sounds exciting, right?"

Houdini lowered his head as if to say yes. Tom hadn't been as excited about a full day of manual labor in a long time. Maybe ever. He knew the reason was more about the woman than the work, and that was just fine with him.

He finished up in the barn just as his phone rang. "Jace, good morning."

"Hey, brother, you sound way too chipper for a weekend."

"Had to get up early today. Got a home improvement project this morning." Tom and Jace had never discussed women, not really. Jace had had more success in that department, both as a teenager and an adult. Tom preferred to listen to his brother talk about Wendy than volunteer any information on his own pathetic love life.

"Did you ask Wendy to marry you?" he asked.

Jace sighed. "Not yet. She's been busy at work, and I haven't been able to get into town to see her, what with Dad's foot and all."

"How's he doing?"

"It's a hairline fracture, but the pain is real." Jace lowered his voice with each word. "I got him to commit to staying off of it on weekends, but that means I have to pick up his slack."

"I'm glad you're there, Jace."

"Me too. And that's most of the news. We go to the doctor again next week. Dad said he'd wear the boot until then, another major victory."

Tom smiled into the brightening sky as he left the barn. "Maybe Dad's going soft in his old age."

"Maybe Dad's in a lot of pain," Jace said.

They laughed together, and a rush of longing to see his dad, hug his brother, raced through Tom. "Okay, well, call me next week and let me know how things are going with both Dad and Wendy."

"You got it."

Tom hung up, his heart on the heavy side because his family lived so far away. *Please keep them safe*, he prayed as he walked. *Help my dad's foot heal quickly.*

Tom climbed the steps to his cabin with the soft reassurance that though he couldn't be in Montana to help his father and celebrate with his brother, that God knew of them and was watching over them.

He felt the same way about himself. God was leading him toward something, but he wasn't sure what. He paused on his porch and glanced over his shoulder toward the barn. He thought of Houdini inside, and Peony, and Hank, and Squire's old horse Juniper.

Tom loved those horses. He loved ranching. But he didn't feel like he'd found the right place to settle permanently. Fear bolted through him. If he wasn't supposed to be at Three Rivers, where should he be?

The wind whispered between the cabins, and Tom thought he heard *cowboy* in Rose's delicate voice. He *was* a cowboy. Always would be.

He pushed into his cabin, worried that maybe being a cowboy wasn't what he should be. That there was something else for him, and he just didn't know what yet. Again, he asked the Lord who he was. And again, he didn't get a definite answer.

An hour later, Tom knocked on Rose's door. She answered this time, only seconds after his fist had landed on the wood.

77

"Mornin'." He grinned at her and scanned the length of her body. She wore an old T-shirt that hung off one shoulder and a pair of workout pants. Tom yanked his eyes back to hers when he realized he was staring too long. "Wanna open the garage so I can unload the flooring?"

She glanced to his truck parked in the driveway. "You said you'd come get me before going to the hardware store."

Tom ducked his head so his hat covered his eyes. "I lied. I couldn't help stopping there first. Besides, we have a ton to do today, and the store's on the way here."

She pushed his shoulder playfully, sending a shockwave right to his heart. "All right, cowboy. I'll get the garage open."

She followed him down the steps to the driveway, where she bent to lift the door.

"I could've done that," he said. "I thought you had an electronic opener."

"I do," Rose said. "It doesn't work. See why this was a priority?"

Kissing her suddenly seemed to be Tom's top priority, but he turned to his truck and heaved a box onto his shoulder. "I called Mike again. He got back to me this morning. He said he can send someone out to measure the door next week."

"Perfect," Rose said. "Do I need to be home?"

"No." Tom set the box near the stairs leading into the dining room. "He said he has returns he's trying to get rid of. Half price."

Rose sucked in a breath. "Half price?"

"And he said he'll throw in a new electronic opener for free."

She smiled, squealed, and launched herself into his arms. He barely caught her, but when he did he never wanted to release her.

"Thank you, cowboy," she whispered. Her fresh scent tickled his senses, drove his pulse to pounding.

"If you get this excited about a garage door, I can't wait to see how you'll react when I tell you about my landscaping guy."

Rose pushed away from him, panic and hope pouring from her eyes. "Landscaping? Tom, no." She shook her head. "We didn't talk about that at all. It's not even on my list."

Tom stepped past her, a streak of determination firing through him. "Well, it's on mine. I'll fix your yard." He flashed her a smile before he got another box of flooring from the truck and hauled it into the garage. She watched him bring in all the boxes, something churning beneath her silence.

When he'd finished, he started up the steps to enter the house. "C'mon, Rose. We have tons of work to do today."

"I can't afford to pay someone for landscaping," she said, refusing to budge. "Mari and I will do it."

Tom shrugged and smiled. "Okay." He opened the door and went through it, sure Rose wouldn't be able to stop him from sending Vince over. She worked during the day, and Vince's boys could have a yard her size cleaned up in a few hours.

Tom knew—he'd called Vince on Wednesday night and set it up for Monday morning. He and Vince had met the first day Tom moved to Three Rivers, before he even had the job at the ranch. Tom had worked for Vince, mowing lawns and trimming hedges and pruning trees, until he got the cowhand job.

Tom had helped Vince out of a spot of trouble, and Vince owed him. His sons were older now, and the five of them would descend on the yard with their professional tools—something Rose and Mari could never do.

"Mornin', Mari," he said to the little girl as she entered the kitchen. "You're not even dressed. How are you gonna help me with the cabinets?" He folded his arms in mock annoyance.

"Tom." A smile slipped into place. "Hungry."

"Oh, all right," he said. "Eat first. But then you've gotta get dressed. I can't stain by myself." Warmth filled his chest as he watched her pull a box of cereal from the cupboard. The heat intensified when Rose stepped next to him.

"Thanks for coming," she said. "I wouldn't even know where to start."

"With emptying the cabinets," he said. "You got the boxes from the bank?"

"Yes." She hooked her thumb over her shoulder. "They're in the living room."

He went with her and carried a few empty boxes into the kitchen. They were medium-sized, just like she'd claimed. "This is what checks come in?"

"Yeah," she said as she opened a cupboard and began removing cooking spray and spices. "We have tons of boxes every week."

"Next time I move, I'll know who to talk to about boxes."

She paused in her work. "You're moving?"

"No," Tom said, starting on the cereal cabinet. A sense of foreboding hung over him, and he knew—he wasn't going to be at Three Rivers permanently. For how much longer, he didn't know.

He swallowed back the rising discomfort, the swirling questions, and got to work. Staying busy had always served Tom well, and by the time they had the cabinets empty, Mari had changed and was ready for a lesson on staining.

He got her doing that, and then he started taping off the ceiling so he and Rose could paint. At the end of the day, they'd accomplished everything he'd hoped they would. Cabinets stained. Walls painted. Tile ripped out.

His back ached as he took a couple of Rose's leftover boxes and slit the tape keeping them together. He laid them on the floor. "You walk on this," he told Mari as he knelt in front of her. "I'll come get the floor in next week."

"Next week," she echoed, looking straight at him. She didn't make much eye contact, and Tom felt the mood in the kitchen sober. Mari flung her arms around his neck and held him in a tight, awkward hug.

He patted her back a couple of times, not quite sure what to say or do. Mari released him and stepped carefully on the boxes to get to the fridge, where she pulled out a box of chocolate milk and retreated to the living room to watch TV.

Tom stood and dusted off his hands. Vince was coming Monday to do the yard. Mike was sending someone next week for the garage door. As he surveyed his work, an overwhelming sense of pride rose to his throat.

Rose deserved a sanctuary in her life. And he was going to make sure she got it.

Chapter Six

Rose pressed into the wall just beyond Tom's sight as he hugged her daughter in the kitchen. Mari didn't give affection that often— hardly ever. And yet there she was, talking to Tom, and hugging Tom, and doing exactly what Tom said.

Rose's heart swelled until she felt like the Grinch. Like her heart had been three sizes too small and she was just now realizing it.

All her personal pacts shattered. She wanted Tom in her life. Not just for her, but for Mari too.

She waited until Mari moved past her—not even seeing her standing in the hall—and went into the living room. Then she stepped into the war zone that had become her kitchen.

"I guess I'll be eating a lot of take-out," she said, hoping her voice didn't give away her spiraling emotions.

"Everything still works," Tom said. "Ollie said the appliances would be coming on Thursday. He said he'd call you to arrange a time to let someone in."

"I can come over on my lunch," Rose said. She stood at the window and looked into her jungle of a backyard. She marveled at the events that had led her here. A home remodel wasn't even on her radar until Tom had come over last weekend to fix her pipes.

"Will I see you at church tomorrow?" he asked, and she realized how close he'd moved toward her. Her professional walls flew into place, but she beat them back. She didn't want to keep distance between them, but something nagged at her. Something that told her it wasn't smart to give in to his boyish charms so easily. Something he'd said about moving had her unsettled.

"Yes, we'll be at church." She turned and found him practically on top of her. She pressed back into the sink as he gazed down at her.

"Can I sit by you again?" He lifted his right hand to her face, but balked before touching her.

She leaned into the near-touch, giving away too much. "Sure," she managed to say.

He gave her a closed-mouth smile and turned away. "See you then." He left through the garage exit, and a moment later, she heard the garage door groan as he pulled it down.

She couldn't take a full breath when she heard him call, "I'll fix this garage door."

His statements about fixing things sounded a lot like declarations of affection, and Rose held her breath until she heard his truck roar to life and then fade into silence as he drove away.

The next morning found Rose restocking the cabinets. A swarm of bees lived in her stomach, buzzing nervously about sitting next to Tom at church. She'd let Mari stay up late watching movies, and she hadn't gotten up yet. Maybe they just wouldn't go to church today.

Rose finished by putting the bowls and plates back in their proper place, breaking down the box, and tossing it into the pile she'd made in the garage. She stood in her kitchen, admiring her newly stained cabinets and trying to imagine what the space would look like with the upgraded appliances she and Tom had selected.

A flowing feeling of peace overcame her and tears sprang to her eyes. As much as she'd fought Tom on this remodel, she did want it. She was glad she'd gotten the loan and could learn how to do home improvement repairs for the future.

Sometime later, Mari woke Rose, who had lain down on the couch and fallen asleep.

"Mom, I'm hungry."

Rose sat up, blinking and trying to figure out where she was and what time it was. When she saw the time, she knew she'd never get herself and Mari ready for church in time. The bees quieted, a sensation that brought relief and regret.

"Mom," Mari complained from the kitchen. "Scrambled eggs."

Rose heaved herself off the couch and went to help Mari make scrambled eggs. She got out the milk, the eggs, and the salt. She set a bowl next to the ingredients and pulled a whisk from the drawer.

"Okay, your turn," she told her daughter.

Mari looked at her, then the eggs, and shook her head.

"Yes, Mari. You can make this by yourself. Remember we just crack the eggs in the bowl and whisk." Rose picked up the kitchen utensil and mimicked the movement.

Mari set her jaw and folded her arms.

Rose copied her. "If you want to eat, you can make it." She sat at the counter and kept her eye on Mari, who steadfastly wouldn't look at her.

"Just crack the eggs, baby," she said.

Mari relaxed, reached for an egg. Time seemed to slow into calculated movements as Mari cocked her hand back and threw the egg at Rose.

She ducked, and the egg smashed against the door leading to the garage. Rose stared at the yolky mess for one, two, three heartbeats as they accelerated. She spun back to Mari at the sound of another *crack!*

This time she'd targeted the cabinets. The newly stained cabinets. A brown tinge accompanied the egg as it ran down the cupboard door.

"Mari," Rose growled. "Stop it."

"Cracking the eggs." Mari grabbed two eggs this time and launched them at the cabinet next to Rose's head. She scampered away from the projectiles and hurried into the kitchen to get the ammunition away from Mari.

Still, Mari managed to get off another egg, this one hitting the corner of the cabinet next to the sink and sending shells and whites in a spectacular shower of muck.

Rose tucked the egg carton under her arm like a football and stared at Mari. "What has gotten into you?"

"I don't want to make eggs."

Rose couldn't look away from her daughter. "Well, there's a lot of things I don't want to do, and I have to do them anyway." She shoved the eggs back in the fridge a little too forcefully. But her blood hummed like wasps, and she felt the pressure behind her eyes building. "Now you'll have to clean up this mess before you can eat."

"I'm hungry."

"So am I!" Rose shouted, regretting the volume of her voice as Mari flinched. Rose hated that she'd snapped, hated that her patience had been so thin to begin with.

She took a deep breath and put another foot between her and Mari. "I'm going to take a shower. When I get back, I want every shell and every egg cleaned off my new cupboards."

Mari didn't answer as Rose strode away. Her hands shook as she washed her hair, as nightmares about what she'd find in the kitchen when she returned ran through her mind, as she contemplated what she could've done differently to keep Mari from launching eggs through the house.

She took her time dressing, drying her hair, and even applying makeup. She noticed Mari's closed bedroom door when she entered the hall, felt the silence envelop her as she snuck toward the kitchen.

The eggs remained. Now dried, the yolks had turned a mustardy yellow. Rose leaned against the wall and sighed, tears coming to her eyes. She let them fall as she went to her new sink and filled it with sudsy water.

If Mari was a normal pre-teen who'd thrown eggs and hadn't cleaned them up, Rose would march her out here and demand she do it. But Mari was as stubborn as the day was long, and no amount of yelling or persuading would work.

As Rose scrubbed the mess from her cabinets, the stain streaked—much the same way her constant flow of tears traced tracks down her cheeks.

Monday morning brought relief. Mari showered and dressed and said nothing about the eggy incident. Rose dropped her off at school, supremely glad she didn't have to deal with the sullen girl for the next nine hours.

She filed paperwork, and met with customers, and ate her sub sandwich in the park. For a few minutes, she pretended like she was a normal mom, with a normal child. She watched toddlers zip down slides and moms try to get their kid to take one more bite of their burger before they went to play.

She thought about calling Tom just to hear him tell her she was a great mom again. She certainly didn't feel like one. But her phone remained in her pocket. He hadn't called yesterday, though she hadn't thought to call him until evening, when Mari finally came out of her room looking for something to eat.

Rose had left the kitchen while she was there, certain she'd have another disaster to clean up afterward. But Mari had made herself a sandwich and was happily watching TV as if nothing had happened.

The bees in Rose's stomach had turned to vipers. Vipers that struck at odd times and made her feel queasy. Why hadn't Tom called?

She felt foolish calling now. Besides, Mari had a riding appointment that evening, and she'd have to face him then.

That's probably why he hasn't called too, she told herself as she made her way back to her office.

The afternoon hours passed too fast, and too soon Rose found herself pulling into her driveway. She did a double-take as she took in the front yard.

"This isn't my house...." Embarrassed, she put the car in reverse and began to back out. She slammed on the brakes again. "Wait a second." She peered through the windshield. The numbers were right. The garage door was the same.

"This *is* my house." She leapt out of the car and stared at the immaculate lawn. Trimmed to what was sure to be exactly one inch, it was aerated and a bright, spring green. The trees on the edge of her property had been trimmed, all the dead foliage on the ground cleared away.

The bushes that ran under the windows in the front had been hedged, and new bark covered the ground in all the beds. New flowers lined the sidewalk leading to the front door.

Disbelief tore through Rose with the force of a tornado. She hurried up the stairs and through the front door. "Carlie!"

The woman who picked up Mari and looked after her came out of the kitchen. "Hey, Rose."

"Did you see the yard?"

"Yeah, it looks great. Mari's out back with Paprika." Carlie put on her jacket and picked up her purse. "See you tomorrow."

Rose didn't even answer. "The back...." She sprinted through the living room and into the kitchen. The backyard rendered her speechless. What once had been a jungle had now been tamed. A gravel path led from the patio to the back fence, where a bird feeder sat. The gravel continued around the edge of the yard, providing a perfect place for Paprika to take care of her business.

The grass had received the same treatment as the front yard, with the dead spots filled in with sod. The fence had been painted red, and a new row of rose bushes decorated the flower bed along the back of the house.

Rose could only stare, blinking as she tried to take it all in. She watched as Mari romped across the grass with Paprika in tow. Mari wore a big smile, and Paprika's tail blurred from side to side, an obvious representation of their joy.

Rose took a breath as if she'd been underwater for a long time. Her chest felt tight, her legs weak. She managed to move through the dining room and into the garage. She paused on the threshold of the backyard, still not quite believing this was her house, her yard, her daughter.

"Mom," Mari called. "Come play."

Rose couldn't resist Mari when she spoke with such enthusiasm. In those rare moments, she saw the child beneath the disorder, the girl she yearned for Mari to be all the time. Rose half-laughed, half-wept as she stepped into the yard with her daughter.

The egg episode from yesterday seemed like it had happened a lifetime ago as they took turns throwing a ball to Paprika. Behind the smiles and laugher, a stream of thought ran through Rose's mind. A stream of thought that featured one person.

Tom.

Tom rode Houdini, gently nudging the horse closer to Juniper, who moved the way Reese directed her.

"Good," Tom said, trying to keep his focus on this therapy session instead of letting it wander to the one immediately following it: Mari's.

"You think Garth will let me come on the round-up?" Reese asked. "I'm ready, Tom."

"I'll talk to him again," Tom promised. "You are ready, Reese."

"I know I'm not a cowhand, but I think going out on the range would be a good challenge for me."

"I agree." Tom didn't have to guide Houdini around the corner. He plodded along a few inches from the fence, steady as can be. "Has Pete's grant come through?"

Reese grinned. "Yeah, didn't he tell you? Came through this mornin'. I'm Courage Reins' new receptionist."

Tom chuckled and glanced toward the main office of the equine therapy program. "You're not a receptionist."

"My main tasks are to answer phones, make reminder calls, and set appointments with clients. What would you call that?"

"You're the...operational director." Tom slid his friend a smile. "I'm glad you'll be out here more often."

"Me too," Reese said. "I'm tired of bagging groceries and hoping to win the lottery."

Their session ended, and Tom helped Reese down from the horse. Reese had improved so much over the past eighteen months that Tom barely recognized him from the man who'd been Pete's first client.

He still walked with a severe limp, but the point was that he walked. He'd left his wheelchair behind months ago, and he'd finished his business management degree online in December. Pete had included him on his latest grant renewal, and Reese finally had a way to support himself and have a real career.

A quick stab of jealousy dove through Tom. He reminded himself that he'd chosen ranching as his career. He could be something else if he wanted. Problem was, he didn't know what else to be.

As Reese brushed down Juniper, Tom heard the crunch of gravel under tires. His heartbeat settled in his stomach, which suddenly rebelled against what he'd eaten for dinner.

"Mari's here," Reese said.

"Yeah." Tom took a couple of steps toward the front of the barn. "See you tomorrow, Reese."

"Later."

Tom's footsteps landed heavily as he went to greet his next client. He'd coached himself not to react to Rose, not to immediately question her, not to judge too quickly. Pastor Scott had spoken of forgiveness yesterday, a service Tom would've liked to have attended with Rose. A service he'd *asked* her to attend with him.

Something must've happened, he told himself for the thirtieth time.

The excuses he made for her had reminded him of the ones he used to make for his mother. He'd expected Rose to call, to let him know why she hadn't shown up at church. But she hadn't, and Tom couldn't help relating her behavior to his mother's. She'd never called either.

Rose emerged from her run-down sedan, her bronze skin and dark hair instantly throwing Tom off his game plan. He wanted to run to her and pepper her with questions to ensure she was okay.

Their eyes met, and held, and Tom felt like he hadn't seen her in months. She combed her fingers through Mari's hair and said something to her. The girl moved forward, her face brightening when she saw Tom loitering in the barn's doorway.

"Tom," she said.

"Peony's waitin' for you." He thumbed behind him. "Reese is back there. Get him to help you saddle her, will you? I want to talk to your mom."

Mari continued past him, and Tom faced Rose again. She had closed half the distance between them, and he watched as she wiped tears from her face.

He moved toward her, abandoning all his plans. "What's wrong?" He took her shoulders in his hands and examined her like her wounds were on the outside. He should know better by now.

"What's wrong?" She hiccupped and swiped at her cheeks again. "You cleaned up my whole yard, that's what's wrong." She stepped back and he let her go. "I told you I couldn't afford that, and it was just so unbelievable, and kind, and—and—did you know I pulled into my driveway and thought I'd made a mistake?"

Tom didn't know what to say. He'd forgotten about Vince's crew taking care of Rose's yard today. His entire thought process had focused on why she hadn't shown up to church when she said she would.

"I haven't seen the yard," he said. "It's nice?"

"Nice?" Rose threw up her arms in frustration. "It's gorgeous!"

"And you're mad about that."

"Yes." She frowned. "No. I—the yard is great. I wish you hadn't done it." She narrowed her eyes at him. "Wait. If you haven't seen it, who did the work?"

Tom stuffed his hands in his pockets. "I have a friend who owed me a favor. He happens to own a landscaping company."

"Vince Howard?"

"You know Vince?"

"He banks with us." Rose stepped closer to Tom, and much as he wished it wouldn't, his throat narrowed at the nearness of her, the clean scent of her skin. "I approve his small business loans to buy his industrial equipment."

"Then you know how he managed to get your yard in shape in only a few hours."

"I can't afford him."

"He owed me a favor. Now we're square."

"But now *I* owe *you* a favor."

Tom cocked his eyebrows and grinned. "I can live with that."

"Tom—"

"Why weren't you at church yesterday?"

Her expression changed in a single blink, and Tom found

weariness and worry in her eyes.

"We were supposed to sit together," he said. "I had to sit alone, and I missed the first part of the sermon because I was waiting for you." He wished his voice hadn't sounded so strangled.

She ducked her head, and though he'd told himself over and over not to push her, not to accuse her, he found the words spilling from his mouth. "I waited outside like a loser for a long time. You never came. I thought for sure you'd call or at least text. You never did." He took a step forward and placed his fingers under her chin, forcing her to look at him.

"So, Rose, I need to know why you didn't show up."

When she remained mute, a vein of apprehension clouding her eyes, he stepped back and paced away. Did he trust her enough to tell her?

She'd trusted him enough to confide in him.

"I have a confession." He kept his back to her. "You want to hear it?"

"Yes," she whispered.

"When I was seven years old, my mother was supposed to come pick me and Jace up from school, just like she always did. She didn't come." His voice turned hollow, his words almost sounded practiced. "We waited on the bench outside the school for what felt like hours. Finally, my dad came and took us home. He said Mom must've just gotten caught up at work. But later, we found out that she'd never gone to work that day. She never came back. I haven't seen her since."

He turned and faced her, finding tears in her eyes he wanted to wipe away until she never had a reason to cry again.

"When you didn't come to church yesterday, I felt abandoned. It's probably stupid, and doesn't make sense to you, but that's how I felt. So I want to know why you couldn't come." He stepped closer to her again, nerves and attraction and a dozen other emotions sparking through him. "I'm sure there's a good reason."

She reached up and touched his face, cradling it in her palm. "I'm sorry about your mom."

Tom's jaw hardened, and he couldn't bring himself to say it was okay. He hadn't realized how deeply his mother's abandonment had cut until yesterday.

"I'm sorry about church too," she said. "Mari wanted scrambled eggs for breakfast, and I've been teaching her how to make them. I said it was her turn to try, and she got mad." She focused on something on Tom's right. "She threw eggs all over the kitchen. When I scrubbed the yolks off the cabinets, the stain smeared and now my kitchen is ruined."

Tom blinked at her, sure he'd heard wrong. "She threw eggs?"

"At my head."

"Rose." Saying her name revealed everything he'd been feeling, and he gathered her into his arms. She clung to him, and one piece of his life fell into place. A terrifying yet comforting thought occurred to him: Being with her felt right.

"I'll fix your cabinets," he whispered into her hair, and she gripped him tighter.

A couple weeks later, Tom didn't even knock as he entered Rose's house. Their weekends had become so routine, he expected to see her sipping coffee at her kitchen counter—a new, granite counter he'd been able to buy at a wholesale price because it wasn't a continuous piece. The seam wasn't noticeable, as he'd placed it right along the sink.

Mari usually slept late on weekends and padded into the kitchen for something to eat close to eleven.

Tom poured himself a cup of coffee from Rose's new machine and joined her. "Carpet's in. We can go get it this morning."

"You didn't stop on your way over?"

"Nah," he said. "Thought you might like to go with me."

She nudged his shoulder with hers. "Thanks, cowboy."

He gave her a smile and slipped his hand into hers. Holding hands with Rose wasn't new. He'd been doing it at church for a couple of weeks now. In the backyard while Mari played with Paprika. In his truck when they drove to the hardware store for supplies. But every time he touched her, something in his chest caught and a measure of contentment whispered through his mind.

"So the painting is done. The kitchen is beautiful. We need to get the carpet installed in the living room and hang the drapes. Then it's on to the main bath. Have you thought about what you want in there?"

"What I want?"

"Yeah, you know. Color palette. Textiles."

"I leave those things to you."

"I thought you might like some more input this time."

"I love what you've done with the rest of my house. I'll love the bathroom too."

Tom took another sip of his coffee, the question he'd been practicing suddenly butting up against the back of his tongue. "Rose?"

"Yeah?" She put her mug down and placed her hand on their entwined fingers.

His mind blanked. His well-rehearsed speech completely gone. "You want to go to dinner tonight?"

"With Mari?"

Tom shook his head. "Reese said he'd come over so we could go out alone." He'd done it—he'd said "go out" to Rose. Out loud.

"See, it's the spring round-up next week, and I know Mari will be gone then, but so will I, and I—well, I want to go out with you." His neck felt so hot, and he mentally commanded himself to stop speaking.

Rose smiled and leaned closer. She reached up and fingered the brim of Tom's cowboy hat. "My spaghetti is disgusting, is that it?"

"Totally disgusting," he deadpanned. "The three plates I ate last weekend almost killed me."

She threw her head back and laughed, revealing a slender neck Tom wanted to kiss. "So no Italian tonight."

"Is that a yes?"

"Do you need me to say yes?"

"Yes."

"Then yes."

Tom leaned down and pressed his lips to her temple, taking a deep breath of her cottony freshness. "I'll go call Reese." He stood and retreated to the backyard, every muscle in his body tight with giddiness.

"Hey, Reese. She said yes." Tom grinned as he said it and couldn't stop, even after he hung up, returned to the kitchen, and Rose asked him why he was smiling so much.

Chapter Seven

Rose enjoyed the warmth of Tom's hand in hers as they made their way to the pick-up counter at the hardware store.

"Carpet's in, right Dale?" Tom leaned against the counter and checked behind them, watching Mari as Diane helped her get a bag of popcorn.

"Yeah, came in last night. It's around the back. You have your truck?"

"Yeah," Rose answered for Tom as he glanced at her and back to where Mari still stood at the popcorn machine. "We'll pull around," she answered as Tom dropped her hand and strode back to the cash registers.

She thanked Dale and followed Tom at a much slower clip. She shouldn't let Tom take care of Mari and her problems, but Rose hadn't had a break in weeks, as Ed had cancelled Mari's last weekend. As far as things stood right now, Mari would go to Amarillo with him next weekend, but Tom would be gone also.

"That's all you get," she heard Tom say. He reached his hand toward Mari, waiting for her to take it. "C'mon, Mari. Let's go look at the fish."

Several seconds passed, and Rose feared her daughter would have a public meltdown over popcorn, as if Rose didn't keep the pantry stocked with Butter Blast. Slowly, with her eyes still fixated on the popcorn machine, she slipped her hand into Tom's and allowed herself to be led away.

Tom snagged Rose's hand in his free one. "We have time for looking at fish, don't we?"

"You're the one with the schedule, cowboy."

He chuckled and squeezed her fingers, leaning down to inhale her hair. A surge of emotion bled through Rose at the tender way he seemed to adore her.

"I like it when you call me cowboy," he murmured just before Mari pulled him down the pet aisle.

"Goldfish," she said, and Tom dropped Rose's hand to crouch down and show Mari the fish she liked.

Rose loitered near the end of the aisle, watching Tom interact with Mari. She admired his steadiness, how nothing seemed to ruffle him. His patience was endless, as she'd seen several times over the past few weeks of working with him in her home, and the many months she'd watched him work with the horses and clients at Courage Reins.

Rose's fingers wandered to her lips, and she thought about kissing Tom that night on their date. She appreciated his strong spirit, something she'd felt at church these past few weeks. Rose felt inadequate sitting next to him, as he seemed fully absorbed in the pastor's lessons and she was just trying to make it through the time.

Tom spent precious minutes with Mari, and another wave of inadequacy rolled over Rose. She never took time to get on Mari's level, talk to her about something simple like fish, or grass, or the drawings she did in the dirt.

She turned away from the scene in the aisle, her heart pounding in her ears as the ever-present tears threatened to overflow. She pushed them back, determined not to cry over Mari again. She'd managed her emotions for several days, especially after meeting with Doctor Parchman and expressing some of her concerns.

He claimed Mari hadn't been acting out of character and that the pre-teen issues she was having seemed amplified because of her Autism. Rose had nothing to compare it to, and nobody else to ask, so she trusted Doctor Parchman and kept trying.

Maybe not as hard as Tom, she thought, but as she turned back and saw Tom straightening to show Mari a tiger shark she realized he wasn't trying at all. He was simply being who he was.

And she liked who he was a lot.

"Reese," Mari said when she opened the front door. "Come in." She stepped back the way Rose had coached her, and she waited silently while Reese limped into the house.

He whistled. "Wow, this place looks great." He took in the freshly painted walls—a medium gray Tom had insisted would compliment the dark carpet he'd chosen. He'd been right.

Rose squished her toes into the soft fibers of the carpet, which had taken them most of the afternoon to install. She didn't know someone could look so good wearing kneepads, but Tom had made them downright desirable. Heat stained Rose's cheeks as she thought about going out alone with him.

"Special instructions?" Reese asked, drawing Rose away from her fantasies.

"She can stay up and watch a movie," Rose said. "She can have popcorn and I bought soda too. She knows how to make Ramen noodles, or scrambled eggs, or there are bagels in the drawer. She can do it all."

"Bed by ten," Tom added. "Otherwise, she doesn't get up in time for church."

Rose swung her attention to him, her eyes wide.

"What?" he asked. "I don't like it when you guys miss church."

"Yeah, because then he has to sit with my ugly mug." Reese laughed and settled heavily on the couch. "What should we watch, Mari?"

"Cartoons," she said, kneeling in front of the cabinet that held the DVDs.

"I like cartoons," he said to her. "I got this." He waved to Tom, who took Rose by the elbow and guided her toward the garage.

"You wearin' those shoes?" Tom glanced at her ballet flats.

"Yes, why?"

"You can walk in them a ways?"

"Sure." But her feet suddenly didn't want to move; she didn't want to leave.

"It's okay," Tom said, tugging her forward again until they stood in the garage. "She'll be fine. We might even be back by ten."

"We might?"

Tom shrugged, his eyes darting left and right—anywhere but on her. "I don't know. This might be a disaster."

Surprised at the self-conscious tone of his voice, Rose glanced at him. "Well, it's nice to know you're human."

He took off his hat and ran his fingers through his hair. "What does that mean?"

She pressed the button to lift the garage door. It smoothly slid up, causing a smile to thin her lips. "It means that you're practically perfect. You're never late. You like church. You know how to stain, and paint, and install carpet. You can tame any horse. I'm not even sure you realize how wonderful you are." She moved toward the driveway, assuming they'd take his truck. He hadn't looked at her car yet. Hadn't even brought up the problems she had with it.

He caught her hand in his as they exited the garage. "You think I'm wonderful?"

She nudged her shoulder into his chest. "Duh, cowboy. You think I go out with everyone who asks?"

"Who's askin'?" he growled, and Rose tipped her head to the sky and laughed. She felt free for the first time in months, maybe years.

Tom helped her into the cab of his truck before going around the front. By the time he'd climbed in behind the wheel, Rose had scooted over to sit right next to him. He started the truck and put his hand in hers.

"So what are we doing tonight?"

Tom turned toward her as if encased in quicksand. It wasn't quite dark as the days were getting longer, but still dusky enough to create an atmosphere of romance. Rose felt heated under the weight of his stare, felt the length of his leg next to hers, the warmth and strength in his fingers.

She gazed up at him, her pulse and her mind running in circles. If he'd just lean down....

He cleared his throat. "Dinner?" His face turned ruddy. "Wherever you want to go."

Rose tore her gaze from his lips as her stomach growled. "Dinner sounds great. I like anything I don't have to make and clean up."

He chuckled and flipped the gearshift into reverse. "It's karaoke night at Paul's. Squire and Pete say they have the best wings in town. You ever been?"

"Mari and I don't go to sports bars much." She leaned her head against his shoulder. "But I like wings."

He turned toward downtown. "How's your singing voice?"

"Terrible." She giggled, and squeezed his fingers. "I bet you have a beautiful voice."

"I'm not bad."

"I'll say," she mumbled under her breath.

"What was that?"

"Nothing." She leaned forward and switched on the radio. A country tune vibrated through the speakers. When she settled back into the seat, Tom's arm slipped easily around her shoulders.

Part of her wanted to snuggle into him, and the other part needed to maintain more distance, at least for a little while. The irrational side won, and she relaxed into his side.

They arrived at the sports bar in only a few minutes, and Tom pulled into the parking lot. He didn't move too fast, or seem stuck in slow motion. But everything about Rose felt just a little bit off. He extended his hand to her, and she seemed to take forever to slide across the seat and to the ground.

His hands landed on her waist as she found her footing. He quickly stepped back, releasing her, and turned away. She thought she heard him mutter something like, "Take it easy, cowboy," but she couldn't be sure.

She also didn't want him to take it easy. So she caught up to him and threaded her fingers between his. "Everything okay?"

"Yes." He clipped the word out and continued with long strides.

"Well, you're practically running," she said. "Could you slow down so I don't have to sprint to keep up?"

He froze, his shoulders tense and his jaw tight. All at once, he relaxed as if all his muscles had turned soft. "Sorry, Rose. I—" He glanced at her.

She saw the adoration in his gaze, and it warmed her from head to toe. She ducked her head and smiled, studying his cowboy boots.

"I told you this might be a disaster." He took off his hat and ran his free hand through his hair. "I'm not very good at this kind of thing."

"You're doing fine, cowboy." She reached up and cradled his face in the palm of her hand. Slowly, so slowly he could block her if he wanted to, she reached for the brim of his hat. It came off easily, and she lowered it to her side as she took in the beauty of his face, the rugged lines, the dark chocolate-colored hair.

"Feels like a disaster," he said, his lips barely moving. "And we haven't even gone inside yet."

"When's the last time you went out with someone?"

"Can I have my hat back before I answer that?" He shifted uncomfortably.

"Why?" she teased. "So you can tuck it low over your eyes so I can't see them?"

"Yes, that's exactly why." A slow grin crossed his face and he lifted his hand to tuck her hair behind her ear. "I feel exposed without it."

Rose lifted up onto her tiptoes and used one hand to brace herself against his broad shoulder. Balanced there, nearly eye-level with him, she pressed his hat back onto his head. "There."

He placed one hand on the small of her back and the adjusted his hat with the other. Once he was satisfied with its position, he ducked his chin, his breath drifting across Rose's face. She sucked in her breath as he moved a hair closer.

Headlights washed over them, and Rose practically jumped backward. She knew almost everyone in town, and what would people say if word got out about her kissing a man in the parking lot of a sports bar?

With the worry came a flash of frustration. She was allowed to go out. Allowed to kiss handsome men. Allowed to be in public.

She just didn't want anyone to know about her relationship with Tom quite yet. She wasn't sure what her relationship with Tom was quite yet.

"You comin'?"

She turned away from her thoughts and found him waiting for her near the entrance. He gestured for her to come with him. She gave him a tight smile as she stepped past him and into the restaurant.

Loud music and some of the worst singing she'd ever heard met her ears. As she latched onto Tom in this new environment, she at least knew she wouldn't be the worst singer in the bar tonight.

Tom kept Rose on his arm as they waited for a table. She clapped her free hand against her thigh when the karaoke song was fast and swayed next to him when it was slow. She smiled and laughed and cheered. She was nothing but polite and genuine and absolutely the most beautiful person he'd ever met.

His feelings kept him silent, his free hand tucked in his pocket. He'd only realized he had feelings for Rose a few weeks ago, and yet each day that passed where he didn't tell her how he felt, where he didn't kiss her, felt like a lost opportunity.

He wouldn't be able to see her for a couple of weeks, and he was determined she'd know how he felt before the night ended—a task that made his throat dry and his vocal chords quiet.

When they finally got called for a table, Tom was glad it was located in the overflow section of the restaurant, where it was quieter and less rambunctious.

"Whew." Rose exhaled as she slid into her side of the booth. "If I'd known karaoke was so much fun, I would've come earlier."

"You like it?"

She glanced around the sports bar. "Yeah, it's so…alive." She smiled at the waitress and grabbed the tall glass of water she'd set down. "I, well, we don't get out much, and when we do, it's never somewhere like this." She met Tom's eyes for half a second before letting her gaze flit somewhere else as she drank.

He couldn't look anywhere but at her, and he again mentally coached himself not to blurt out something embarrassing tonight.

"Heard anything from Ed?" he asked.

She shrugged. "He's in Washington this weekend. I guess it's his third interview, which is a big deal." She placed her elbows on the table and leaned into them. "But I decided to stop worrying about it."

Tom's eyebrows shot up. "You did?"

Desirable pink splotches shone in her cheeks. "Yeah. Remember last Sunday when Pastor Scott was talking about the future and how we shouldn't be afraid of it? I decided to do that."

Her eyes flashed with fear, with a bit of embarrassment. Tom gave her a lazy grin, hoping to calm her. "I didn't know you listened to Pastor Scott."

She folded her arms and leaned away from him. "What does that mean?"

He picked up his own water and took a long drink. "It means I can feel you staring at me during the whole service."

Color stained her whole face now. "I'm not used to having help at church," she said. "And you keep Mari quiet. I need something to pass the time." She shrugged, obviously trying to make light of her staring. "And I can obviously listen and watch you at the same time."

"So you admit to watching me."

"Do you need me to say yes?"

He couldn't hold back the huge grin that split his face. "Yes."

"Fine." A smile twitched in the corners of her mouth. "Yes."

Tom chuckled and reached across the table for her hand. "I like looking at you too." He ducked his head to hide the emotion he felt scampering through his bloodstream, sure she'd be able to read everything in his expression if she could see it. "And I'm glad you decided to listen to Pastor Scott." He sighed. "I'm trying to do the same thing, but I'm obviously not as brave as you."

The waitress arrived, saving Tom from explaining. They ordered, and the karaoke in the other room quieted.

"Why aren't you as brave?" Rose asked.

The restlessness that had been plaguing Tom for the past few weeks surged. "Have you ever known something in your life wasn't quite right, but you didn't know what, and you didn't know how to fix it?" He looked openly at her, trusting her with this part of his life.

"Maybe. What's going on?"

Tom shifted in his seat, unsure of what to say. He hadn't been able to identify things quite yet. "I don't know. I feel...lost. Like maybe I shouldn't be here in Three Rivers, like maybe being a cowboy isn't what I should be doing with my life."

"Tom." Rose squeezed his hand. "You're the best cowboy I know. Courage Reins would be nothing without your help, and

LIZ ISAACSON

neither would the ranch." She cocked her head to the side. "So what's really going on?"

He shook his head. "I don't know. I've been listening really hard in church these past several weeks, trying to figure out what God wants me to do, and I still don't know." He glanced toward the doorway when the karaoke started again.

Rose pulled her hand back when the waitress arrived with their food. They watched each other until she moved away. "I'm sure you'll figure it out," she said. "Anything I can do to help?"

Tom picked up a chicken wing. "You're doin' it, beautiful."

She blushed and the conversation moved to lighter topics. She'd barely finished her last French fry when a woman stepped up to their table. She held a mic toward Rose, who blinked at it like it was a serpent.

"Go on," Tom said, settling back in the booth, as content as he'd felt in many days.

"Tom, no," she hissed, trying to pass him the mic.

"Can't, honey," the woman drawled. "I have to pick another woman."

"I can't sing," Rose tried.

"Go on," Tom said again. "I'm sure it's not that bad."

Rose shot him a glare that could melt metal before snatching the mic and sliding out of the booth. Tom watched her go, a smile on his face at the fiery Latin side of Rose.

He spilled from the sports bar with Rose on his arm, both of them laughing. He couldn't stop, and he couldn't breathe. He felt drunk of this woman, her scent, her fearlessness.

"You were so right," he said once he'd found a way to laugh and breathe at the same time. "You really can't sing."

"I was fine until that last note."

"No." Tom tucked her into his side as they headed toward his truck. "No, beautiful, you really weren't." He chuckled again, simply because happiness flowed through him.

She climbed in the truck before him, leaving him barely enough room to sit behind the wheel. "Where to now?" she asked.

He gazed down at her, her face shadowed beneath his hat. "I was thinking of something else you don't get to do much because of Mari."

"Oh yeah? What's that?"

"It's a little unorthodox." Tom swallowed and sent a prayer heavenward. "But there's a wildlife conservatory on the west side of town, and they have a night hike every weekend. Thought you might like to do that."

"Is that why you asked me about my shoes before we left?"

"Maybe."

"Sure. Sounds fun. And you're right. I would never go night hiking with Mari."

Tom drove through town and pulled two flashlights from the glove box after he parked. They signed in and found themselves part of a very small group of hikers. The guide introduced himself as Neil, and he led off along the stream with another couple behind him, and Tom and Rose bringing up the rear.

Tom slipped his hand into Rose's, wondering how long he'd be able to hold her hand before the path narrowed or the terrain steepened. He enjoyed the wind rustling through the grass, as it reminded him of being out on the range.

"It's nice here," he said. "Peaceful."

"Mm." Rose paused when the guide did and listened to him speak about the hill they'd be climbing, and some of the wildlife they'd see on the trail.

Tom's heart stuttered, stalled. "Snakes?"

"We have seen some snakes," Neil said. "But nothing to worry about. If there are any, we'll see them, as they usually crawl out onto the paths as the sun goes down to get as warm as possible. They won't be hiding in the grass."

Tom nodded like everything was fine, but tension made his muscles tight, tight, tight.

"What's with you and snakes?" Rose asked.

He walked on wooden legs, suddenly back on that trial, back in those woods, back with his company.

"I served in the Army once," he said as the terrain got a bit steeper. "We had a drop zone trial, which basically means they drive us blind out into the middle of nowhere and leave us there with only our packs. We have to figure out where we are, and how to get back in only seventy-two hours."

The path narrowed, and Rose moved in front of him. She hiked slowly, which allowed the other couple and Neil to move ahead. Tom appreciated the buffer of privacy she'd created for him.

"On the morning of day two, we knew where we were. We knew

where base camp was. We only needed to cover forty miles, so we set out early. It was still pretty dark. I was walking in the back half of the company, my eyes on the south side of the path, watching for unfriendlies."

Tom could smell the early morning dew, the sagebrush, the sweat of the other men. He forced himself to take a breath, to remove himself from the memories.

"I heard someone yelling from up front, but it wasn't until I got there that I realized they'd been bitten by a snake." The sound of a rattler strike buzzed in his ears, and no matter how much he shook his head it wouldn't stop.

"I hung back." His voice sounded so far away, like he was living the memory through wax paper. "I heard a rustling in the leaves, and I turned. It was then that I realized no one had caught the snake. The pain from the bite was quick, sharp. I remember yelling, and I remember someone pulling me to my feet, and I remember the swish of a knife and the scent of blood."

Tom paused, though the path continued. He suddenly didn't want to take another step. A rustle to his left sent a bolt of fear through his body. The sound battered around in his skull.

"Tom?" Rose appeared in front of him, her deep, dark eyes full of concern.

"My company got me back," he whispered. "The other guy too. But it turns out I have a severe allergy to snake venom. My commanding officer recommended I request an honorable discharge from the Army, as vipers are common in the Middle East." His voice sounded like he was speaking into a box.

"And did you?"

Tom shook his head. "I couldn't. I didn't want my dad to think I'd quit." He shrugged as the life returned to his limbs. He hadn't felt this sluggish since the snakebite. "My commanding officer filed the paperwork, citing I had a weak immune system as well as the allergy, and I was discharged. Never got to be deployed."

Bitterness coated his throat, much as he tried to swallow it away. He knew he should be happy he hadn't had to fight overseas. Hadn't had to leave his loved ones behind. But the truth was, his discharge—honorable as it may have been—only served to remind Tom of his shortcomings.

"I'm sorry," Rose said at the same time Tom said, "Let's catch up to the others."

He didn't want her pity, though she didn't seem to have any in her eyes. More like understanding that he hadn't been able to have what he wanted. As he followed her to the crest of the hill, he knew Rose understood that concept better than anyone.

"Take a look around," Neil said as they arrived. "We'll be up here for about a half hour before going down. The moon is a waxing gibbous tonight." He grinned at the two couples and moved to a rock overlooking the prairie.

Tom gazed into the sky, a peaceful feeling settling on his shoulders. Rose snuggled into his side. "I love the moon," she said. "It reminds me that there's something bigger out there, something more than me, something powerful and amazing."

"Yeah." Tom watched the other couple move to the edge of the path and look over the town. "Which do you want to see? The range or the town?"

"Town." Rose led him to the left, where the twinkling lights from Three Rivers winked up at them. "We haven't come that far," she said as they stood side by side gazing at the town. "Probably only a mile, and it still feels like the town is really far away."

Tom agreed, his nervous energy over reliving his snakebite ebbing into the night. He appreciated that this silence wasn't strained, that he could be himself with Rose and he didn't have to make excuses for why he didn't seem to have a lot to say.

"Thank you, cowboy," she whispered. "You're right. I never would've done this on my own."

He wove his arm around her back, threaded his fingers through her belt loops, and turned her toward him. "Thank you for sayin' yes." He swiped his cowboy hat off his head with his free hand and lowered his mouth to hers.

She received his kiss instantly, and Tom felt like the ground beneath him had disappeared. The tips of her fingers caught in his hair, sending lightning to his scalp, his shoulders, his jaw, everywhere she touched.

He kept a tight hold on her waist as he deepened their kiss, never wanting this night to end.

Chapter Eight

Rose thought for sure her lips would be bruised, but as she looked at herself in her bathroom mirror, she couldn't tell a difference between her reflection now and the one she'd checked just before leaving for dinner.

Liar. She smiled at herself. There was a marked difference in the woman she saw now. That woman looked happy, healthy, harmonious. She looked like someone who'd just been kissed so thoroughly that all other men would be measured against that kiss forever.

And the man of her affections still sat in her living room, jabbering with Reese over the status of the first baseball game of the season.

Tom.

Rose grinned just thinking about him. About the tender yet strong way he'd kissed her under the stars. The way he'd pressed her into the driver's side of his truck and kissed her before driving her home. The passion in his eyes, his touch, his lips when he'd stopped her in the garage for one final kiss before they entered the house.

It seemed that now that he'd kissed her, he couldn't stop. And she didn't want him to stop. He'd been real with her, honest about the questions he had, open about his time in the Army. She hadn't known he'd served, and she understood why he didn't tell anyone.

A noise beyond the closed door of the bathroom startled her. She stepped into the hall and switched off the light in the bathroom, her gaze immediately drawn to Mari's closed door.

Mari.

Ever-present, she should always come first. And she would, Rose knew that. But it was nice to know that she could go out for a few hours and not be burdened with constant worry over her daughter.

She stepped into the living room, where she only saw one cowboy lounging on the couch. Tom stood, swiping his hat off his head when he saw her. "Hey."

"Hey." She glanced toward the front door. "Did Reese leave?"

"Just barely. Said to tell you he'd love to sit with Mari again. That she's easy company."

Jealousy jumped through Rose. Sitting with Mari had never been easy for her. "I'll text him thank you." She reached for her phone, but Tom caught her wrist, bringing it slowly to his lips.

"Church tomorrow?"

She nodded, her eyes locked with his as his touch burned through her body. "Thank you for tonight." Emotion clouded her voice. "I had such a great time."

"Me too." He gave her that cowboy smile she loved so much and stepped into her personal space. "Can I kiss you one last

117

time?"

"Do you need me to say yes?"

Tom gave her a soft, sweet smile. "Not this time." He leaned down and matched his mouth to hers. It fit perfectly, and Rose wondered how she'd lived before kissing this cowboy. If she had, she realized now that it wasn't a life at all.

Early Monday morning, after chores but before the team left for the annual spring round-up, Tom breathed in deeply through his nose as the call connected and the line started ringing. And ringing. And ringing.

He wasn't surprised. His dad had probably gone out to complete his own morning chores, and he hadn't entered the twenty-first century with everyone else and didn't carry a cell phone.

"Come on, Dad," Tom mumbled. A wash of guilt flowed through him for not calling earlier, for staying in the South for so long without visiting. His dad understood—he was a rancher too, and the work didn't stop so men could take vacations.

"Hello?" His dad's gruff voice came through the phone, and relief filled the empty places the guilt had scrubbed clean.

"Dad, it's Tom." He took another breath. "How are you?"

"Tom." His tone took on a friendly edge. "I'm doin' just fine, son. How's Texas?"

And just like that, Tom knew his dad didn't hold an ounce of blame for him not visiting. "It's great, Dad. Already headed into summer. Jace said you hurt your foot."

"Oh, it's nothing."

Tom imagined the wave of a callused hand as his dad spoke. "Jace worries too much. I've been up and about just like normal."

"I'm sure you have." Tom stared out the back window of his cabin as the sun brightened the sky, trying to gather strength from the range. "But Dad, you fractured your foot. Surely it hurts a little. You should take it easy."

Jace had called last night, and though he hadn't asked Tom to call their father, Tom knew his brother was at the end of his rope. Claimed their dad hadn't slowed down at all, and yes, Jace worried he'd do more damage.

"Went to the doctor last week. He cleared me," his dad said.

"Okay," Tom said. "I'm just worried about you." His throat narrowed. "Maybe I could get away and come visit for a bit." He worried his thumbnail between his teeth, trying to work out when he could leave Three Rivers for a couple of days. Definitely not until after the round-up.

The thought of going home to Montana sang through him, and Tom released his tension. "I'm headed out on the annual round-up today. Won't be back until next Sunday. Once we get caught up around the ranch after that, maybe."

"Oh, wait a few more weeks," his dad said. "It's still frozen here, and you've never liked ranching in the winter." He chuckled, and Tom joined him, glad his dad hadn't said he didn't need to come at all.

"What's it looking like up there?" he asked. "Still drifts everywhere?"

"Mostly. But then there's the mud."

Tom groaned. "Maybe I'll wait until summer." They laughed again, and Tom's heart lifted with the easy conversation with his dad. With his conscience reassured and a plan in place to visit soon, Tom hung up and headed out to the horse barn to start organizing the cowboys.

Later that afternoon, Tom kept an eye on Reese and Arrowhead, the calmest working horse on the ranch. Peony wasn't used to week-long round-ups, and while Reese had gotten permission to come on the excursion, he couldn't ride Peony. But Arrowhead, a even-tempered Altai with more points on his black spots than rounded edges. He could walk or run for days, making him the best horse for the round-up.

Satisfied that Reese was happy and well, Tom went back to squinting at the horizon. They'd left the cabin in section eight an hour ago, and still had another couple of hours before they'd reach the edge of the ranch where the cattle wintered.

Letting Houdini dictate the course, Tom's mind wandered, as it often did while out on the range. The cowboys didn't speak much, choosing to let their horses spread out. Tom particularly enjoyed his time with only Houdini's soft snuffling and the prairie wind for company.

At least he had until very recently. Now, his mind seemed consumed with thoughts of his father, of Montana, of Rose Reyes.

He sighed, thinking of how easy his life had been before he's started seeing Rose with different eyes, before he'd started renovating her house, before he'd kissed her.

You wouldn't take that back, he told himself as a gust of wind kicked up over a swell and threatened to unseat his cowboy hat. Kissing Rose had been magical, and though he'd seen her at church the day before, he felt like he needed to see her again. Everyday. So he could help her with Mari, and take her to do things she wouldn't normally do, and kiss her afterward.

"Hey, there." Garth came up alongside Tom, riding a tall tan horse name Peanut Butter.

"Garth."

"How's Reese doin'?"

Tom didn't glance Reese's way, instead choosing to cock an eyebrow at Garth. "How do you think he's doin'?"

"Looks good to me." Garth peered into the distance, where Reese rode near Ethan and some of the other boys.

"He's a good rider. Thanks for lettin' him come. He needs this for his confidence."

Garth lowered his chin in acknowledgement. "I reckon we better talk about Juliette."

Tom's stomach twisted, and he swallowed. "What for?"

"Well, see, she and I—well, I guess I just want to know a couple of things."

Tom eyed his boss. "What do you want to know?"

Garth took a deep breath. "Why won't she go out with me?" The words exploded from his mouth all at once, like he'd been holding them in for a long time.

"She won't? You asked?"

"'Bout ten times," Garth said darkly. "We've been gettin' along just fine. She seems happy, let me hold her hand at church, that kind of stuff." He focused on the horizon, his expression hooded. "Then she said something about not bein' able to finish what I start or some nonsense."

Tom couldn't tell if Garth was more flustered by Juliette's rejections, more frustrated, or more furious. He wore his hat low and suddenly the range needed constant scanning to ensure they didn't get off course.

"I didn't know you were interested in Juliette," Tom said. "We've been goin' over there for a while."

"She makes a mean barbeque," he said, as if that alone qualified a woman as desirable.

"No wonder she won't go out with you." Tom chuckled. "Her best quality is her cooking?" He tipped his head back and sent a laugh to the sky.

"No," Garth growled. "And can you keep it down?"

Tom contained his laugher but not his smile. "So what do you need me for?"

"Why is she like that?"

"Like what?"

Garth lifted the reins in his hand as if shrugging. "Resistant."

"I don't know," Tom said. "It's not like we talk about her troubled past or anything."

"She has a troubled past?"

"Garth," Tom said. "I don't know. I was a kid; I didn't pay

attention to what my aunt was doing. She left Montana over a decade ago." He slid him a sideways glance. "Have you asked her?"

"I would if she'd go out with me." The desperation in his voice made Tom sit a little straighter in the saddle.

He cleared his throat. "Okay, so she grew up on a ranch in Montana. Maybe she's not interested in the ranching lifestyle?"

Garth muttered under his breath and glanced away.

"And...my dad didn't have it so lucky in love, and maybe she doesn't want to get hurt too." He grinned again. "Or maybe she thinks you're too old for her."

"Hey!" Garth swung toward Tom. "She's older than me."

Tom laughed again, unable to contain it. "I know, I know." He sobered at the anguished look on Garth's face. "I didn't realize you liked her so much."

"I didn't either. But since she turned me down, she's all I can think about."

Tom contemplated his boss. "You know, Juliette can smell a lie from a hundred yards out. She knows when someone's serious and when they're not. Maybe she just doesn't think you're the real deal."

He frowned. "Why would she think that?"

"I have no idea. But the real trick is getting her to change her mind." He clucked his tongue. "That's not gonna be easy. If there's one thing I know about Juliette, it's that she's as stubborn as a mule."

"Great," Garth muttered, nudging his horse forward. "I'd appreciate it if you didn't mention any of this to anyone." He rode ahead before Tom could answer, before Tom's soft chuckle escaped his lips.

Chapter Nine

Rose made it through the week by merely holding on by her fingertips. Holding on to the fact that this weekend, she'd be home alone. No construction. No home improvement. No Mari complaining about the way Rose had cut her apple.

When Ed came on Saturday morning to pick up Mari, he sent her out to his truck alone. A cluster of wings beat in Rose's chest. "How did the interview go?"

A smile stole across his face so fast Rose barely saw it. "Good enough. I should know soon, Rose."

She rubbed her hands up her arms as if cold, but she wore a long-sleeved shirt and didn't have a chill. "Just let me know, Ed."

"I wanted to talk to you about something else."

"Okay."

"I'm getting married in October." He glanced over his shoulder and out the door. "I haven't talked to Mari about it. I'd like your help with that."

Rose's mouth turned into sand. She tried to swallow away the unpleasant texture, but her tongue felt too heavy.

"Maybe when I bring her back tomorrow afternoon," Ed said.

"Tomorrow afternoon's fine," Rose said. "You realize she won't react well to it. She resists change."

Ed sighed and wiped his hands down his face. "I know, Rose. She's my daughter too." He turned and pushed the screen door out, leaving it to crash closed behind him.

She's my daughter too.

What did that mean?

Rose moved to the doorway and lifted her hand in a good-bye wave for Mari. She didn't return it. Rose closed the front door and leaned against it, the silence of the house speaking to her, calming her.

Just like she had last week with Tom, she felt free. And with that freedom came a pocket of guilt she couldn't rid herself of. She wondered if she would ever be able to live without feeling guilty about something she'd said to Mari, something she'd done to try to help Mari, something she'd felt about Mari.

But this was her weekend, and she wasn't going to spend too much time worrying about Ed and Mari. Oh, no. Rose had plans.

Her first stop of the day was at the salon, where she'd booked a full spa experience. The sun shone merrily overhead, and her car didn't give her much trouble on the way there. Her sister texted about the upcoming birthday party for Mari just as Rose arrived at the salon.

She smiled at the exuberance she could hear in Fiona's words, though she was only reading the message. She fired off a quick response and set her phone to silent. She was going to get a pedicure, then a facial, and then a massage. She had plans to pick up pizza on the way home and then spend the evening with her favorite rom-com.

She relaxed into the massage chair while her feet soaked, closing her eyes to fully escape.

"Morning, Rose," a woman said, and she jerked her eyes open to find Leslie Allan, the mother of a girl with Down syndrome who went to the same academy as Mari.

"Hi, Leslie." Rose smiled at her. While she probably could've shared her worries, her fears, her frustrations with Leslie, she never had. Leslie had a husband at home to help. A husband who ran one of the doctor's offices in town. A husband who hadn't left.

"Mari's gone with Ed this weekend?"

"Yes." Rose sighed as the nail technician began sudsing up her feet. "I decided I needed a little pampering. It's been a rough couple of months."

"How's she doing with the horses?"

"Oh, I forgot Lucy went out to Courage Reins too."

Leslie's enthusiasm faded a bit. "We haven't been going quite as much."

Rose frowned. "Why not? She didn't like it? It wasn't working?" Rose adored the program at Courage Reins, and curiosity threaded through her as to why Leslie wouldn't take Lucy as often as possible.

"She loved it," Leslie said. "But she loved Brett Murphy. He was the only one she would listen to."

"Ah," Rose said. "And he's not there anymore."

Leslie leaned back into her massage chair. "He left last summer for a deployment, and then he moved to North Carolina with his wife." She lifted her foot out of the water so her technician could begin. "Don't get me wrong, I'm happy for him. But Lucy…she can be impossible about some things. If she knows she has an appointment, she'll cry the whole day. If I don't tell her, and try to drive out there, as soon as she realizes where we're going, she screams." She let out an exasperated sigh. "So I've sort of given up on it."

"What about another assistant?" Rose asked. "Maybe they'd come to your house, get acquainted with Lucy."

Leslie smiled at her. "I should ask Pete about that."

"Mari loves her assistant. His name's Tom." Rose's voice caught on Tom's name, but Leslie didn't seem to notice.

Leslie reached over and clasped her hand around Rose's. "Thanks, Rose." She closed her eyes and fell silent, something for which Rose was grateful.

After several hours of rest and relaxation, Rose stopped by Papa Henry's to pick up her pizza. On a whim, she decided to order a second pie and swing by Vince Howard's place to tell him thank you.

"Better make it two extra pizzas," she told the clerk as she thought about Vince's crew of teenage boys. She wasn't sure why she'd thought of Vince at this moment, or why she wanted to say thank you these several weeks later. She just had a feeling she didn't want to ignore.

When she climbed the steps to knock on the door, she heard a man shouting. Her feet froze, but somehow she managed to raise her hand and knock. The angry voices inside quieted, and a moment later one of Vince's sons opened the door.

"Hi," she said. "Um, is your dad here?"

"Dad!" The brown-haired boy turned back to her and waved her in. "You want to come in?"

"No, no." She lifted the pizzas. "I just wanted to tell him thank you for the work he did on my yard."

Vince came around the corner, his eyes curious—until they saw her. "Rose, come in."

"No, I can't stay," she said. "I—I just wanted to bring you dinner as a thank you for what you did in my yard."

Confusion rode his eyebrows as he took the pizza boxes. "Your yard?"

"Tom Lovell said he arranged with you to clean up my yard. I'm sure you remember it." Rose grinned. "The one that looked like a jungle?"

"I've seen worse." Vince chuckled and passed the food to his son. "Take that to Mom. Well, thank you, Rose. You sure you can't come in?"

"No, I have to get home." She hoped he wouldn't ask anything more, and he didn't. Rose continued home, ate her pizza, and watched her movie. The only thing that would've made a better Saturday would've been Tom by her side, his lips on hers before he disappeared into the dark.

Rose tipped her head back and closed her eyes before sending a note of gratitude to the Lord for sending him into her life.

Tom whistled to Winston, who brought in the left side of the cattle with the expertise of a dog who'd participated in a dozen round-ups. Tom felt a rush of appreciation for his black Lab, for returning to a soft bed after sleeping on the open range or in a cabin with a dozen other men for six nights. He used the last of his energy to brush down Houdini and make sure the horse had what he needed.

With his thoughts tangling about making the visit to Montana more permanent, he climbed the steps to his cabin, unlocked the door, and dropped his pack just inside the living room. He yawned, every cell in his body screaming for sleep.

He set a pot of coffee to brew and stepped into the shower, making it as hot as he could stand. He scrubbed and scrubbed until the stink of horse was gone, and he dressed in a comfortable pair of sweats before heading out to the kitchen for a cup of coffee.

His phone chimed, drawing his attention to where he'd left it plugged in on the kitchen counter. He never took his cell out on the range, because he couldn't get service anyway. The cowboys carried radios, and they didn't go out alone, so he never needed it.

Flipping it over, a blue light at the top flashed violently. He swiped it open, and saw several missed calls. One from Rose—his lips curved into a smile—and four from Jace—his stomach fell to the floor.

His coffee mug stumbled as he tried to set it down and didn't quite succeed. Hot liquid splashed over the side, burning his hand.

He barely felt the pain. He stared at his phone as if through a layer of wax paper, imagining the worst possible scenario.

Something had happened with his dad. Maybe his foot wasn't healing right, despite the doctor's clearance.

Something happened with Wendy. Maybe she'd said no to Jace's proposal.

He pressed his eyes closed and sent a prayer for strength to endure whatever had happened. To support his brother as best as he could.

He dialed Jace, who hadn't left a message.

"Jace," he said when his brother answered. "What's going on?"

"Where have you been? I called over and over."

Tom's defenses rose. "It's the annual round-up. I was out on the range."

A heavy sigh came through the line. "I'm sorry, Tom. Really. It's just I've been here alone, and I'm stressed out." He spoke faster with every word. "It's Dad. He was out checking the herd and his horse got spooked. It threw him."

Threw him.

Threw him.

Threw him.

The words echoed endlessly. "Dad doesn't get thrown," Tom said, his voice belonging to someone else. "And Duke doesn't get spooked."

"Tom, Duke retired last year. Dad has a new horse now. And he did get spooked, and Dad did get thrown. He's in the hospital."

Tom sucked in a breath that seared like ice in his lungs. "Is he awake?"

"He managed to make it back to the homestead before he lost consciousness. He's woken up a few times over the past twenty-four hours. The doctors seem to think that's good."

"Twenty-four hours? When did this happen?"

"Yesterday morning. Tom…you might want to come home." Jace didn't say anything more. He didn't need to.

Fear and desperation warred in his stomach, rising until his throat felt stuffed full of cotton. "Jace?"

"Soon," he said. "I'm sure you have details to work out. I'll let you go. Let me know if you can come. I'll send someone to the airport to pick you up." Jace exhaled. "I've already called Aunt Juliette. She said she can't get away from the clinic."

"Okay." Tom hung up and stared at his phone, wondering when it had become an object he didn't want around.

It rang again, and he startled away from it, further spilling his coffee.

Rose's picture and name came up on the screen, and he swiped open the call. "Rose," he said, but again, he didn't recognize his own voice.

"Tom?"

"Yeah." He ran his hand over his eyes, half wishing he'd gone to bed before checking his phone. He wasn't sure he'd be able to sleep now, especially if he had travel plans to make.

"Did you get my message?"

"No," he said. "I've been home for about a half hour, and all I've done is shower and make coffee." *And find out my dad might be dying.*

The world seemed too heavy. The air too dense. Everything felt scrambled inside Tom's heart and mind. Should he go home for a few days? Or forever?

The thought startled him, but it wasn't the first time he'd had it. He'd felt unsettled in Three Rivers for a few weeks now, something that grated against his comfortable life, his good job at the ranch, his new relationship with Rose.

"Oh, well, I got some bad news—I guess. I don't really know if it's bad news or not, and I wanted to talk to you about it." Rose paused, and Tom tried to make her words line up in his head, but they just swam around like frenzied fish.

She started speaking again, but Tom couldn't listen. He closed his eyes and tried to focus.

"Tom?"

"Can I come over?"

"Sure."

He hung up and pulled on a hoodie before heading over to Garth's. He knocked and knocked. At least five minutes passed before the man opened the door. "Tom," he growled. "Why aren't you in bed?"

"My dad got thrown by a horse," he said. "I need to get up to Montana as fast as possible. Can you manage without me on the ranch for a few days?"

Garth's eyes rounded and the growl disappeared from his eyebrows. "Yeah, of course. Go."

Tom nodded and descended the steps, his eyelids heavy as he

made the drive to Rose's house. Possibilities for his future whirled through his mind, but Tom honestly had no idea what he wanted to do with this situation. Or with his job. Rose seemed to be crystal clear to him, but the possibility of a lasting relationship with her seemed distant, especially if he left Three Rivers for good.

What should I do? He cast his eyes toward the ceiling of his truck as he drove, listening for an answer.

Go home entered his mind, and he flexed his knuckles around the steering wheel.

Chapter Ten

Rose stood at the living room window, waiting for Tom to arrive. When his truck's headlights finally cut a swath through the darkness, she moved to the front door. She had it open before he'd put the vehicle in park.

She hadn't meant to call and leave him an anxiety-ridden message. But he said he hadn't listened to it, and he'd seemed distracted and distant on the phone. One look at his face, and she saw the weight he carried.

"What's wrong?" She moved down the front steps and met him on the sidewalk. Exhaustion troubled his eyes, and worry rode in the set of his mouth.

He gripped her shoulders and drank her in, his eyes sparking with emotion. "Is Mari with Ed?"

"No, she's inside watching TV," she said, wanting to tack on a dozen sentences about how she and Ed had spoken to Mari about his upcoming marriage, the fit Mari had thrown, the long hours Rose had endured with Mari since.

And of course, Ed got to go home to his pretty fiancée and leave Rose to deal with the aftermath. She was so tired of watching Ed leave, watching his back as he walked away, watching his tail lights as they returned him to his normal life.

Rose didn't get such luxuries.

Tom pulled her into a hug, and she wrapped her arms around his strong shoulders—shoulders that now felt more vulnerable though they didn't tremor. "My dad is hurt. I have to go home to Montana tomorrow."

"Tomorrow?" Rose hated the shrillness in her voice. She hated that she'd looked forward to his return because maybe he'd take care of Mari, at least for one hour. Tears sprang to Rose's eyes, for his father, but more for herself. She hated this selfish streak she possessed, wondering what she'd need to do to be cured of it.

"Can I use your computer?" He stepped back and looked over her shoulder. "I need to make travel plans." He pressed his palm to hers and stepped toward the front door. "Will you help me?"

"Yeah, sure." She moved with him, stuffing her complaints and cares to the soles of her feet. The anguish on his face was enough to silence her own worries.

"Evenin', Mari." Tom stepped over to the girl and sat next to her on the couch. "Did you have a good week?"

She swung her dark eyes toward him, and Rose feared she'd scream at him the way she had at Rose. She blinked and turned back to the television screen.

"Yeah, me too." Tom sighed as he got to his feet. "We'll be in the kitchen." He pulled Rose along with a pleading gaze, and she only paused long enough to grab her laptop from the end table before she followed him.

He didn't speak as he clicked and typed. He pulled his wallet out of his back pocket to buy an airline ticket. "When should I come back?" He looked at her with round eyes, and she saw all the way inside him.

Her heart pumped out an extra beat as she saw the depth of her own feelings in his eyes. She immediately pulled back, tried to construct a wall around her heart. He was leaving too.

This is different, she told herself sternly. "How is your dad?"

"I don't really know." Tom removed his hat and scrubbed his hands through his hair. "My brother called and said he was in the hospital and I needed to come home soon. So I'm goin'."

"Did you talk to Garth?"

"Yeah, he said I could be gone as long as I needed."

"Then go for the whole week." Rose placed her hand over his, and he curled his fingers around hers. "The ranch will be here when you get back."

Tom blinked and seemed to look at her for the first time that night. "What about you, Rose? Will you be here when I get back?"

Rose liked the husky edge in his voice, the way his eyes sparkled like dark diamonds. "Yes," she said. "Right here, where I always am." She wished the words didn't come out coated with so much bitterness, but Tom didn't seem to notice.

He didn't seem to notice how quiet she was for the next hour as he finalized his travel plans. Didn't seem to notice that she never told him about the bad news she'd gotten. He never asked either, and later, as Rose watched him drive away, she wondered if that's all she'd ever get in her life: Men driving away.

You're not being fair, she told herself. *His dad is in the hospital!*

But she couldn't shake the jittery feeling in her stomach, the one tapping out that Tom might not come home as quickly as he'd promised.

"Surprise!" Fiona burst into Rose's office, a huge smile on her face.

Rose looked up from her paperwork, beyond shocked to find her sister standing in the doorway of her office. "What are you doing here?"

Fi flounced to the chairs opposite of Rose's desk and flopped into one. "You sounded so down on the phone last night. Decided I'd take the day off and come see my favorite sister."

Her grin felt contagious, and a smile seeped onto Rose's face. "Fi, you're the best. But I'm your only sister."

"So can we go to lunch? I'm starving."

Monday morning had been exceptionally slow at the bank, so Rose abandoned her paperwork and reached for her purse. "Let's go."

Fi linked her elbow through Rose's, and Rose couldn't contain the press of emotion that surged up her throat. "Thanks for coming."

"Oh, don't cry," she said. "You've done harder things than this. Remember when Ed's response to your divorce papers was to stay in Amarillo permanently?"

"He sent a moving company to get his things." Rose shook her head to dislodge the memories. She managed to keep the tears at bay as she said, "This is different. *Mari's* different. She's...." She pushed out of the bank and into the weak April sunlight.

"She's becoming a teenager," Fi supplied.

Horror snaked through Rose's bloodstream. "Yes, that. Nothing with her is easy, or predictable. She's better about some things, like talking to people and doing chores, but she balks completely at things that didn't used to be a problem." She unlocked her car and thought of the yolky mess and ruined cabinets.

Fiona flipped her dark hair over her shoulder after she slid into the passenger seat. "I feel like breakfast. Bacon." She glanced at Rose. "Yes, this definitely requires a lot of bacon. Is there anywhere that serves breakfast all day here?"

Laughter bubbled from Rose's mouth. "You came to the right place if you want to order a plate of bacon." She put the car in reverse, ignoring the shudder she felt in the brake pedal. "I know just the diner we need."

An hour later, Rose's spirits had been sufficiently lifted. Fi had always been able to help her see the silver lining in all things, even when they were kids.

Fiona set down her coffee mug. "So, we haven't talked about your new boyfriend."

Rose's hand went to her lips. "He's not my boyfriend."

Fi tossed a giggle toward the ceiling. "Yes, he is. What's his name again?"

"Tom," Rose said.

The grin splitting Fiona's face widened. She leaned forward and placed her elbows on the table. "And how is *Tooom*?" She made her voice breathy and weak.

"Come on."

"That's how you said his name." Fi laughed again.

"I did not." Rose hadn't realized she'd started saying his name differently. She felt differently about him, that was for sure. She'd missed him more than she thought possible over the weekend, and she had another lonely one looming.

"So?" Fi waved away the waitress when she came by with the coffee pot.

Rose groaned as she pressed one palm to her stomach. "So I think I better lay off the bacon buffet if I want to keep him."

Fiona squealed. "So he's yours."

Rose thought of the starlit kiss, the comfortable way her hand seemed to fit exactly in hers. "I honestly don't know. He seems to adore Mari. And...."

"And what?"

Rose looked openly at her sister. "I honestly don't know if I deserve him."

"Rose." Fiona sobered. "Of course you do." She sat back in the booth, her earlier playfulness gone. "Look at you. Successful career. Gorgeous. Put together."

"You didn't see my yard."

Fi flashed a brief smile. "So you think your worth is dependent on what your lawn looks like?"

"No." Rose glanced out the window to the busy Main Street. "I've never actually considered remarrying. Mari—"

"Mari will be just fine. She resists change, but eventually she accepts it."

"But Ed—"

"This is about you." Fiona leaned forward again, this time her bossy big sister expression plainly in place. "Don't let someone great go just because you're worried about Mari, and definitely don't spend another second thinking about Ed."

Rose nodded, wanting to take her sister's advice, needing to believe she could have a chance at a future that included Tom. But when her phone buzzed with a text from the academy, stating that *Mari was in the principal's office and could Rose sneak over for a few minutes?* a sinking feeling deep down told her the timing for a relationship between her and Tom was simply off.

Tom stared at his phone, sure he'd heard his aunt wrong. "You're really not coming?" He refocused on the road in front of him. He'd driven to Amarillo plenty of times, but never when everything on the horizon seemed so far away. He blinked, but he still felt like he existed behind a film of plastic wrap.

"I can't get away from the clinic," Juliette said. She didn't sound like her normal, confident self. Not a trace of her humor, her good nature. No, she sounded worried.

"I got away from the ranch," Tom said. "And—"

"Look, Tom. I can't go, okay? I don't have to explain myself to you."

"He's your brother!" Tom yanked the steering wheel to the right and pulled off the road. "You should be going to see him, Juliette. He might not—"

"I spoke with Jace this morning," Juliette said over him. "I'm aware of how my brother is doing. Believe me, if I could go to Montana, I would."

The fight left Tom's chest. He wasn't sure why he cared if Juliette came to see his dad or not. Nerves rioted in his stomach as he set his truck back on the road and continued toward the airport. "I'll call you when I get there."

"I'd appreciate that." Juliette sighed. "I'm sorry, Tom. I know this is hard for you, and I'd like to be there to help you. I just...can't."

With her words, Tom realized that the reason for his jitters. He didn't want to travel home alone. Aunt Juliette's presence would've soothed him. "We'll talk soon," he promised before he hung up, wondering if he could've asked Rose to come with him. He dismissed the idea. She had a job and a daughter to take care of.

When Tom deplaned in Montana, he remembered why he didn't get home to visit very often. Flying was for birds, not people, and his ears still ached from the changes in elevation.

He paused, people streaming past him at the Missoula airport. A sense of helplessness crowded into his lungs, pressing against his ability to breathe. He felt forgotten, insignificant, lost.

A woman passed him with a couple of teenagers in tow. "Come on," she said. "Baggage claim is this way."

He followed the woman down the wide corridor to find his suitcase. He didn't see his brother until Jace called his name. Tom turned and his feet slowed at the sight of his older brother. His older brother he hadn't seen in far too long. He strode forward, his heart pounding with pins and needles against his tongue.

"Jace." He engulfed his brother in a hug and clapped him on the back. Tom wasn't normally an emotional man, but everything he'd felt since he'd spoken to Jace last night teemed just beneath his skin, right against his vocal chords. To keep it contained, he didn't speak, just kept a tight hold on his brother.

"Dad woke up this morning," Jace said a few seconds later, releasing Tom and stepping back. "But he was disoriented, and well, the doctors didn't like that."

"What does that mean?" Tom asked as the first pieces of luggage started tumbling onto the carousel.

"They're concerned he's not progressing."

Tom pressed his lips into a thin line as he waited for his bag.

"And, uh, Tom?" Jace cleared his throat and seemed fascinated by the other travelers in the airport. He took off his cowboy hat and raked his fingers through hair the same color as Tom's. The gesture reminded Tom of one he'd done countless times when he was weary, or nervous, or scared. "Mom's here."

The floor vanished beneath Tom's feet, and he staggered, trying to find even ground. Or at least a reality that didn't have his mom in it.

"Tom?" Jace's voice reverberated in his head. "It's going to be okay, Tom."

He shook his head. Seeing his mother after twenty years was definitely not going to be okay.

"Aunt Gwen is coming into town tonight too," Jace said, his eyes cutting to Tom. "She has a flight into Kalispell. She'll meet us at the hospital."

Aunt Gwen, he thought. His mother's only sister, Aunt Gwen was not his favorite aunt by a long shot, but Tom would be civil. He always had been, even when Aunt Gwen had made sharp comments about the Lovell boys not being able to do anything but become cowboys.

Jace had never seemed to mind her comment, but it grated at Tom. He liked being a fifth generation cowboy, and wasn't sure why Gwen cared what he did with his life anyway. Over the years, her words had twisted and become the reason Tom believed his mother had left.

His mother didn't like cowboys. His own mother didn't like *him*.

"Well, come on." Jace moved toward the baggage claim. "We still have a two hour drive ahead of us to get to Gold Valley. Best get your suitcase so we can go."

Jace made easy conversation on the way to Gold Valley, the town where Tom had gone to elementary school, where he'd learned to fish in the creeks, where he'd ridden his bicycle on weekends to buy penny-candy from Luis, the Mexican marketplace owner. He smiled at the memories, loved the way Montana seemed frozen in time.

"Still a fair bit of snow here," he said as they neared the city limits.

"Especially up in the mountains." Jace peered up and out the windshield. "Dad shouldn't have gone up to the higher paddocks."

Tom agreed, but kept quiet. Upon entering the town, a sense of nostalgia washed over him, powering through his tension and bringing a grateful smile to his lips. Peace descended on his heart, light as a feather, and he knew whatever happened with his father, whatever he needed to say—or not say—to his mother would work out.

Nerves crowded his stomach as he entered the hospital, stepped onto the elevator, and entered the recovery ward where his father was. Jace pushed the door in gently, as if something dangerous might be lurking behind it.

"He's asleep," came a raspy whisper, and Tom's heart skipped, stalled. He backed up a step, pushing into Jace as he re-entered the hall.

A thin, honey-blonde woman stepped out of the room, and Tom blinked at his mother as his limited memories returned. He hated that they were still there, filed away in the back recesses of his seven-year-old mind. He hated that he didn't have very many, and that all he had retained seemed stained by her decades-long absence.

"Hello, Tommy." She watched him with hazel eyes, a ring of panic around the irises, her own anxiety evident in the way she wrung her hands and smoothed down her clothes.

He hated that she used his seven-year-old nickname. He hadn't been Tommy since sixth grade. "Laura," he said.

She flinched as if a gunshot had sounded, one foot hitting the door and nudging it open.

"Can I go in alone, please?" he asked Jace. The hallway felt so

145

crowded, though it was wide enough for two hospital beds to pass and only the four of them stood there.

"Yeah." Jace gestured for him to go inside, and Tom squeezed behind his brother so he wouldn't have to get too close to the woman who'd abandoned him. He wished he could be more forgiving, more understanding, more…something.

He heard Jace speak to Laura, but he didn't want to know what they said. He closed the door behind him and gave his eyes a few seconds to adjust to the murky light.

His dad lay in the hospital bed, his eyes closed, with tubes in his nose and wrist. The steady hum of machines and the sharp scent of sterility hung in the air. Tom took a few steps toward his father and found a cast on his right foot and a much larger casing on his left leg. A rod joined the two casts, and Tom's chest felt like someone had jumped on it.

He moved to the bedside and placed his hand on his dad's. "Hey, Dad," he whispered. "It's Tom." He leaned down and pressed a kiss to his dad's forehead. "I can't believe a horse got the better of the best cowboy in Montana."

His dad inhaled, and only his lips moved when he said, "Best cowboy in the west."

Tom half chuckled, half wept. "That's right. Best cowboy in the west."

His dad's eyes fluttered open and took a few seconds to focus on Tom. "Hey, son. It's good to see you."

Tom pulled the only chair in the room closer and sat down. "How you feelin', Dad?"

"'Bout like I look, I imagine."

"You don't look that great." Tom added a half-smile to his statement.

"Broke my hip." He lifted his head and looked at his legs. "That's why the two casts are joined."

Tom nodded though his heart tore a little. He wasn't a doctor, but he knew a broken hip at his dad's age wasn't good. It probably didn't mean death, but it certainly meant retirement and a future of pain every time the weather turned threatening.

"I recommended Jace to be the new foreman at Horseshoe Home Ranch," he said. "There's a vacancy for the controller now, if you want to come home."

Tom stared at his father, the idea of returning to his childhood home bubbling in his brain. Before he could answer, a nurse opened the door and entered the room.

"Good to see you awake, Mister Lovell." She flashed him a smile as she checked the whiteboard mounted on the wall. "Looks like you had meds a couple hours ago." She turned to him. "You feeling okay? I can get you another dose if you need them."

"My leg aches a bit."

"On a scale of one to ten, what would you say it is?"

"Three or four."

Tom knew that a three for his dad was a seven for other people. Normal people who didn't spent forty years roughing it on the range, birthing calves, branding cattle, and hauling hay.

"Let's wait a little longer then." She made a note on the board and headed for the door.

The door clicked closed again and Tom ducked his head as the question he wanted to ask pushed against the roof of his mouth. "Dad, what's Mom doin' here?"

His father sighed, the sound full of one thing Tom had never seen in his dad: Defeat.

"Jace called her. He said it was about time we patched things up as a family. I didn't expect she'd come, but well, she's here."

"And you're okay with her being here?"

"Can't stop a grown woman from doin' what she wants."

Tom couldn't disagree, but he didn't know how to converse with a woman he hadn't seen or heard from in twenty years. As far as he was concerned, they didn't have anything between them to patch.

"What she did to you and Jace wasn't right, and it wasn't fair." His father's hand came down heavy and hot on Tom's, causing him to look up and into his dad's weathered face. For the first time in years, Tom admitted that his dad was old. And he looked it. Tom hadn't seen the aging on a day-to-day basis, and it hit him like a fist to the face.

"But she's here, and I don't think she's looking to make excuses. Laura never was one for that."

"Hmm." Tom had no idea what his mother's habits were, what she did and didn't do. She'd made sure of that when she left and never came back. Familiar bitterness coated his throat, and Tom couldn't swallow it away.

The door opened and Jace poked his head in. "Aunt Gwen just got here. She and Mom want to come in."

Tom stood and smiled at his dad in what he hoped was a

reassuring way. "I'll see you later, Dad. Love you." He turned and edged past Aunt Gwen and his mom as they moved into the room. Once in the brightness of the hall, Tom headed for the exit.

"Gonna go get some coffee," he called over his shoulder. His brother's disappointment was palpable, but Tom didn't slow or go back. He wondered when Jace had known their mother would be there.

He spun around and palmed his way back into the hallway. Jace still faced him, just as tall, just as wide, just as dark. Neither of them seemed to have any of their mother in them.

"When did you know Mom would be here?"

Jace raised his chin. "She answered when I called the first time."

Tom turned away and took a few steps toward the exit. "You could've told me before I got here."

"Didn't think you'd come if you knew."

Tom raised his hand in a dismissive wave and went to get his coffee. Jace's words cut, and they cut deep. Because they were true. Had Tom known his mother would be in Montana, he probably wouldn't have come.

As he nursed his stale coffee in the hospital cafeteria, he wondered what that said about him. It only took him a few minutes to conclude that it wasn't something good. Wasn't what he wanted his brother to think about him.

He left the cafeteria and wandered the corridors at the hospital, turning here and getting in an elevator there. He finally caught sight of a sign that said chapel, and he turned that way. The doors were unlocked and the lights low. No one seemed to be in the small room with only a few pews.

Tom took a seat in the back row and looked up at the stained glass. The waning Montana light barely penetrated the glass, but the beauty still rendered Tom silent, and still. The sensation only lasted a few heartbeats before his troubles descended on him again.

Behind worries of his father's health and future, concern for his relationship with Rose seemed to grow and grow until she was all he could think about. He pulled out his phone and checked his service.

Not great, but enough to make a phone call. The tension leaked from him as the line rang and she answered.

Chapter Eleven

Rose's phone drew her attention from the movie she and Fiona had put in a half hour ago. She'd ended up just checking Mari out of school and bringing her home after her episode at school. Apparently she'd started screaming when her teacher asked her to login to the computer.

"She's done it hundreds of times," the principal had said. "I don't know what's going on with her." The concern in the woman's eyes had prompted Rose to give her the whole story about Ed's engagement, his possible relocation.

She'd felt the need to apologize, but the principal waved it away with a, "Take her home, Rose. She'll be okay."

"Are you going to get that?" Fiona asked, her eyes sliding over the screen. "It's the handsome cowboy."

Rose grabbed for her phone and slipped into the kitchen to answer Tom's call, determined to keep her mouth shut and just listen.

"How was work?" he asked after they exchanged hellos.

"I didn't actually go today," she said, settling at the bar. "My sister came into town for a couple of days, we played hooky."

"Dangerous," Tom said, and Rose got the feeling he didn't really have a lot to say and that his mind lingered elsewhere.

"How's your dad?"

"He's alive," Tom said. "And I don't think he's going to die anytime soon." He sighed, and Rose wished the sound wasn't quite so sorrowful. "But he's older than I remember, and he's going to retire from ranching."

"Where will he go?"

"Oh, we'll never get my dad to leave Montana."

Fear sliced sharply through Rose. She wondered if Tom would move up there to help his dad. "Where will he live? Didn't you grow up on the ranch? Does he have his own house?"

"He bought land decades ago. Been building a place on it for as long as I can remember. Must be done by now." He paused, and she imagined his midnight eyes filled with worry and troubles. "My mother is here. I have…some things to deal with."

Rose didn't want to ask, but the words spilled out of her mouth. "How long will you be up there?"

"I don't know, Rose."

Rose wished she could've gone to Montana with him, but the thought of altering anything more in Mari's life right now brought a sense of panic so keen, Rose felt it all the way to her toes.

"How's Mari? She seemed off last night."

Rose took a deep breath. "You sure you want the whole story?"

"Of course I do." His sharp intake of breath startled Rose. "You had something to tell me last night, and I forgot. It's about Mari, isn't it?"

"Yes." Rose worked to keep the tremor out of her voice. She was tired of feeling weak. Tired of the tears having control over her. Tired of feeling like a victim inside her own skin. She glanced toward Fiona, who wasn't even pretending to watch the movie. Her sister gestured for her to *go on, tell him*. Buoyed by Fi's confidence in her, Rose took a deep breath.

"On Sunday, Ed and I told her that he's getting re-married in October. She did not handle it well, and she's been particularly difficult to live with. Sullen. Moody. Random outbursts of crying or yelling." She moved to the window and looked into her dark backyard, taking the affection Paprika gave her when the dog came over and laid down on her foot.

"She had an episode at school today, and I had to go get her. I'm exhausted," Rose admitted. "And I don't know how to help her understand that Ed won't love her any less, or that he'll still have the same amount of time for her." She had her own doubts about Ed, mostly because of his job status. But she'd never wondered if he loved Mari.

"Take her out to the ranch this week."

"It's not her week to be there."

"So what? Call Pete and make an extra appointment. It'll help. At the very least, you'll get an hour away from her."

"I'll see how she does tomorrow," Rose said. "When she's mad like this, she usually gets over it in a few days. This is just bigger than usual."

"I wish I was there to help you," he whispered.

"Me too." Her own voice came out strangled, and she decided

that meant she needed to end the call. That, or she'd probably blurt something embarrassing, like how much she missed him and wished he could be hers forever. So she said her good-byes and hung up.

Mari did seem better in the morning, but Rose suspected that feat belonged to Fiona, who got up with her, made her scrambled eggs, and helped her with the homework she'd missed the day before.

"Time to go," Rose said, the only words she'd uttered that morning.

"I'm going to head back to Amarillo." Fiona knelt in front of Mari. "You be good for your momma, okay?"

Mari nodded, and Fi placed a kiss on the girl's forehead before standing and dwarfing Rose in a tight hug. "Call me with anything you need, anytime."

"Thanks, Fi." She swallowed back the emotion and painted on a bright smile instead. She'd talked everything through with Fiona—about Mari, about Tom—and she felt better than she had in several long weeks.

Rose's hopes lifted like helium balloons when Mari waved to her before heading into the academy, and she couldn't help smiling on the way to the bank.

Rose got great satisfaction from doing well at work. It was one area of her life she could control, excel, achieve something. She'd begun an income evaluation for a young couple who'd applied for a home loan when her phone rang.

She glanced at it, her stomach swooping up and then down,

before opening the call. "Morning, Ed." She checked the next box on the form before she realized Ed hadn't responded.

Abandoning her work, Rose glanced up to see if her office door was closed. It wasn't, and she got up to shut this conversation off from the rest of the bank.

"I got the job, Rose."

Five words. Five words, and Rose's knees felt weak.

Five words. Five words, and Rose's hope for a stable life with Mari collapsed.

Five words.

"That's great, Ed," she managed to choke out. She knew this job was a promotion for him, a great opportunity with more money and prestige.

"It's in Washington."

"I remember. When do you have to go?"

"We'll move up there by the end of the month, and we have to go this weekend for paperwork, we'll look for a house, that kind of stuff."

Rose pressed her back into the door. "I'll tell Mari."

"I'll call her and tell her everything."

"No." Rose shook her head, her strength pouring back into her muscles. "No, Ed. She can't handle this kind of news in a phone call."

"Well, I don't think I can get to Three Rivers this week."

Of course he didn't. Rose felt like her entire life was spiraling out of control, being turned upside down, pressed inside out, and all she could do was watch from behind her executive desk.

Tom straightened as his mom and Aunt Gwen exited his father's hospital room. He'd just been starting to think he'd become a permanent part of the nurse's station.

"You guys heading out?" Jace asked, telling Tom to back down with a single glance.

Laura squared her bony shoulders. "I'd like to go to dinner with you boys." She kept her eyes on Jace the longest, only sliding her gaze to Tom after the words had settled into the silence of the hallway.

"I don't—"

"Tommy," she said at the same time Jace said, "Yeah, of course. We'll go." He speared Tom with a pleading look, one that begged Tom to drop his anger and at least *try*.

"Great," his mother said. "Gwen is too tired to join us. She'll catch up with you boys tomorrow." She nodded at her sister, who made a hasty exit. Tom had to admit he wasn't sorry to see her go, though the prospect of spending the next couple of hours with his mom "catching up" sounded like the worst form of torture he could imagine.

"You want to drive yourself?" Jace asked as he stepped toward the exit with Laura. "Tom and I are staying out on the ranch. Depending on where we go, we could all go together, and then drop you off."

"I'll drive myself," she said. "I was thinking of going to Migliano's. Remember we went there for your birthday?"

Tom didn't remember the birthday dinner she spoke of, but Jace smiled.

"Was that when I turned seven?"

She nodded and Tom trailed behind them like a forgotten puppy as they made their way out of the hospital and into the parking garage. Resentment that he'd only had seven birthdays with his mother—and he couldn't remember a single one of them—burned through him. He climbed in Jace's truck and exhaled.

"I don't know if I can do this," he confessed.

"Sure you can," his brother said. "It's not forever, Tom. She just wants to be able to apologize in person." He backed out of the parking space.

"Oh, is that why I haven't heard from her in two decades? She couldn't make a phone call, send a card, or message me on Facebook to say sorry? That had to be done in person?"

Jace didn't answer as he maneuvered through town toward the restaurant. He pulled into the parking lot and killed the engine. He stared through the windshield, and Tom waited, having experienced this tactic before with his older brother.

"Jace—"

"Just give her a chance." He held up his hands in surrender. "That's all I'm asking."

Tom searched his older brother's expression, reaching deep down inside himself for that well of peace he'd felt on the drive from the airport to Gold Valley. He'd been sure things would work out with his mother then, and he needed that reassurance now.

"Okay," Tom said. "Let's go."

The wait didn't exist on a Monday night, and they were seated in a booth immediately. Jace and Laura made small talk until the waitress came and took their drink orders.

"Tell us about Texas," Jace said, putting Tom on the spot.

"It's warmer than here." Tom glanced up when the waitress set down his soda. He reached for it, unwrapped a straw, and took a long drag of carbonation.

"I really am sorry," Tom's mother said, getting straight to the point. "I hope you'll be able to forgive me one day."

Tom watched his mother from across the booth, seeing her sincerity. Feeling her sincerity. Wishing he could believe her sincerity for long enough to forgive her.

"Nobody's perfect," he finally said. "I know I'm not." He shot a glance at Jace, daring him to contradict him. "Heck, my own brother thought I wouldn't come home if I knew you were here."

"Tom—"

He held up his hand. "It's fine. I know I moved away and left a lot on your shoulders. I know I haven't come back to visit. I know I need to do better on all that." A slip of guilt pricked his chest. How many more years would've passed before Tom would've come to visit his dad? Five? Ten?

It's not your fault he got thrown, Tom told himself. He was just having a hard time believing it. A wave of exhaustion overcame him, and he focused on the menu. The sooner they ordered, the sooner the food would come, the sooner they could leave.

He let Jace fill the silence with news about the Horseshoe Home Ranch, about Wendy, about anything that didn't stray into their childhood. Tom contributed a little bit about his responsibilities at Three Rivers, but he guarded Rose close to his heart, telling a little white lie when his mother asked if he was seeing anyone.

"Not for a while, no," he said, telling himself that his relationship with Rose was new, and they hadn't had a chance to define it yet.

After the meal, the dessert, the conversation that didn't really tell Tom where his mother had been all these years or why she'd left, he'd had enough for one day. "Well, I'm beat." He cast a meaningful look to Jace. "Should we go?"

Jace yawned and stood. "Yeah, it's another half hour to the ranch." He leaned over and gave his mother a quick hug, but Tom settled for lifting his hand in a good-bye wave.

"I'm staying close to the hospital. So is Gwen." She threw a twenty on the table for a tip. "One of us will call you if anything changes."

Tom nodded with Jace and they left the restaurant. While chatty earlier, Jace didn't seem to have much to say on the way out to the ranch. Tom appreciated the silence, especially after the bustle of the airport, the hospital, the restaurant. After the chaos of dealing with his family, his feelings, his faith.

"If you don't want to work at the ranch," Jace said. "There's that therapeutic riding center at the base of the mountain. Silver Creek. They're always looking for experienced horsemen."

Tom swung his gaze to Jace's side of the truck. "Isn't that a teen rehab center?"

"Yeah. Focuses on equine therapy to help with their recovery."

"How many horses do they have?"

Jace shrugged. "Couple dozen. One of our seasonal cowhands is their groom. Owen says he's always lookin' for help."

"Full-time help?" Tom thought of Rose, and Mari, and if they'd move to Montana to start a family with him. He startled at the thought of having them as *his* family. He liked Rose. Liked looking at her, spending time with her, kissing her. But again, they hadn't defined anything between them.

"Not sure," Jace said, interrupting Tom's spiraling thoughts. "Might be worth looking into."

Tom grunted in response. There were a lot of things worth looking into. Moving fifteen hundred miles north without a job wasn't necessarily one of them. Moving an Autistic girl and her mother wasn't either. Unless he married Rose.

Tom swallowed through the dryness in his mouth. He'd just barely started to get to know Rose. They certainly weren't to the stage where they were talking long-term.

Sure you are, whispered through his mind. Rose wasn't the kind of person to get involved at all without considering the long-term.

"So Dad's going home on Wednesday?" Tom asked to distract himself and steer the conversation into safer territory.

"Yeah. He's got a place on the north edge of town, on the road heading out to the lake."

"It's ready? Electricity? Water? Food?"

"All the utilities have been turned on. Gwen and Mom are going out there tomorrow to make sure it's clean, with towels, food, and all that."

Tom nodded. "And then what?"

"Then we'll help get Dad settled in. You could stay there with him for a day or two, make sure he's getting around okay, eating well, and taking his medication."

Tom mulled over how many days he'd need to stay. "We could move him in on Wednesday, and I'll stay until Friday." The thought of spending the weekend with Rose in springtime Texas appealed to him over taking care of his father in snowy winter-never-ends Montana.

"If you want to leave on Friday, that's fine," Jace said. But his tone didn't convey the same message.

"You workin' this weekend?"

"It's likely. I don't know if I'll be named the foreman, but someone will, and there'll be some changes around the ranch." He turned down the road that led to Horseshoe Home, and Tom wished it were daytime so he could see the ways the ranch had changed, and the ways it hadn't.

Strong memories of racing Jace along this dirt road rooted themselves in his mind. He'd hardly ever won—until that growth spurt in seventh grade when his legs finally outpaced Jace's. He remembered the drifted snow keeping them from school for days at a time, the wicked winds that chapped his cheeks only seconds after he'd left to feed the chickens, the relentless summer sun that beat on the ranch for three good months.

Jace pulled up to a cabin separate from the others. "This is Dad's place. I thought we'd sleep here tonight and start packing things up tomorrow. Mom'll hold things down at the hospital."

Tom got out of the truck and retrieved his suitcase from the back. "Lead the way."

The foreman's cabin had it's own yard, with a fence in the back. A wrap-around porch provided great views, though Tom knew one could get tired of seeing only snow in all directions. Inside the cabin, the overwhelming scent of his father—musky cologne and burnt coffee—met his nose. It also stirred a sense of belonging Tom hadn't experienced yet during his time in Gold Valley.

Jace paced through the living room and into the bedroom in the back. "I'll sleep in here. Is the loft okay for you?"

Tom confirmed that it was, but he stayed near the door taking in the life of his father in this simple cowboy cabin. He'd lived a good life. Forty years working the land he loved, riding horses, and training boys to be men.

Standing in his father's cabin, Tom had the overwhelming sense that being a Montana cowboy wasn't a bad thing. Not a bad thing at all.

Chapter Twelve

Rose employed every ounce of patience she'd been blessed with when it came to Mari. She prepared her daughter's favorite dinner on Tuesday night, and managed to placate Mari in the evening after work.

But she after Mari went to bed, Rose changed into her painting clothes and went into the bathroom to finish the remodel. Tom was supposed to finish it up this weekend, but she wanted to surprise him, show him that she could fix some of her own problems.

She caught sight of herself in the mirror as she set a paint tray on the newly installed granite counter. Tucking a stray lock of hair behind her ear, she noticed how tired she looked. She felt it too, all the way down into her bones.

"Maybe you should just call Tom and forget the painting," she told her reflection. He'd called yesterday afternoon, but Rose missed him. The missing might've been worse than the exhaustion.

She returned to the kitchen and brought her phone with her into the bathroom before dialing Tom's number. He answered on the second ring.

"Hey, beautiful."

Rose smiled at the endearment and the tenderness in his voice. "You sound better tonight."

"I feel better," he said. "How's Mari?"

"She's okay." Rose set the phone on speaker and put it on the back of the toilet. "She's in bed early tonight. I think she's as tired as I am." She gave a light laugh, grateful when it didn't come out strained. "What are you up to tonight?"

"Finishing up the packing at my dad's. We're moving him into his new house tomorrow."

Rose's heart sank into her stomach. "Got a lot to do still? Can't keep me company while I finish painting the baseboards in the bathroom?"

"You're painting the baseboards in the bathroom?"

Rose dipped the slanted brush in the white paint and wiped it on the side of the can like Tom had taught her. "Well, my handsome hired help skipped town, and somehow, painting doesn't get done by itself."

Several beats of silence came through the phone. "Tom? Did I lose you?"

"No," he said. "I was just enjoying how you called me handsome." He laughed, and she joined him, her level of comfort growing.

"How did things go with your mom?" She swiped the paint on the baseboard near the tub, moving in slow, even strokes.

He exhaled. "Good enough. Didn't see her today. By the time Jace and I got to the hospital, she'd left." He spoke with finality, and though Rose wanted to question him further about his mother, she decided to switch topics.

"How's your dad?"

"Good, good. He's getting released tomorrow afternoon. We're hoping to have everything he needs at his new place. I'll be staying there with him."

"He'll be okay on his own? Your mom doesn't live in Gold Valley, does she?"

"No, she's in Missoula. But Jace is here." Tom's voice quieted. "Oh, and Rose, I'm coming home on Friday night."

"You are?" Rose paused in her painting, wondering why her heart had suddenly decided to do a tap dance. He'd be home for the weekend, and giddiness spread through her.

"My mom's leaving that day. My aunt is leaving on Thursday. Jace isn't going back to the ranch until Monday. Dad doesn't need both of us through the weekend."

Rose thought she heard something beneath his words, something hidden in between the syllables. She wasn't sure what it was, couldn't identify it, but something felt off-kilter.

"Let's talk about something else," he said. "Tell me how the painting is going."

"You want to talk about painting baseboards?" She appraised her work. She had almost half the bathroom done in just their short conversation. It didn't matter that it was a small space—she'd fixed it.

"Rose, I want to talk about everything with you."

She sighed, a happy sound full of adoration for the cowboy she wished she could see in person. They continued to jabber about everything and nothing, and Rose finally made it to bed two hours later than she normally did.

But the bathroom baseboards were flawless, and she couldn't straighten the smile from her lips because of Tom's warm voice and casual conversation, his throaty laugh and his flirty words. As she fell into sleep, she realized she was falling for Tom Lovell.

Wednesday morning, Tom found himself elbow deep in unpacking dishes in his dad's new kitchen. Jace had half a dozen boxes in the bedroom, and Tom enjoyed his solitary task of going through the kitchen and setting up what his dad needed in his new place.

He thought of the last time he'd boxed up the contents of someone's cupboards—Rose's cupboards—so he could sand and stain them. His lips curved upward at the thought of her. The ache in his chest seemed endless, and his fingers stumbled over a dinner plate as he realized he missed her.

You love her, entered his mind, and this time he stalled completely in his work. He stared at the flowered plate in his hand, wondering if his mind was playing tricks on his heart. He'd known Rose for a couple of years, had been working with Mari for eighteen months.

But it had only been a few weeks since Tom had looked at Rose with new eyes. Only a little more than a week since he'd kissed her for the first time. Could he really love her?

He practically dropped the plate into the stack in the box, his mind reeling as his heart beat out a new message. *Ro-Rose. Ro-Rose.*

Tom leaned against the counter, more confused than ever. How could he have Rose and Montana? How could he help his father and keep Mari in his life? How could he feel called home to Horseshoe Home and want to stay at Three Rivers?

"You can't always have everything you want," he said out loud, another of his father's life lessons. But his heart and his mind started to work together, and Tom thought maybe, just maybe, with a bit of luck and a lot of prayer, he could have Rose and Mari. And Montana.

Later that day, Tom rode with Jace in his pickup truck as they followed their mom and dad through town. Getting Dad from his room to the car had been a forty-minute ordeal that had caused an argument between Tom's mom and one of the nurses. In the end, his mother had won, and his dad sat in the backseat of her car, his leg extended over the back of the front passenger seat. How they were going to get him up the several steps to his front door, Tom had no idea.

He'd loaded the wheelchair into the back of Jace's truck, but unless he and his brother could lift Dad up the stairs in it, it was useless.

"We should've built a ramp over Dad's stairs," he mused as they made a turn north. His mom drove at the speed of a snail and Tom felt near the edge of his patience.

"We didn't have time for that." Jace glanced at him. "We'll get him inside. He won't be leaving for a while."

Tom grunted in agreement, his mind wandering to Aunt Gwen. She'd gone to the grocery store instead of crowding things at the hospital. Tom wondered if she'd bring home chick food, or something he could actually turn into a meal for him and his dad. Sudden nerves struck him as he realized that once Dad arrived at home and got settled, everyone else would leave. His mom and aunt would get to go back to their hotel. Jace, tired as he was, would likely head back out to the ranch.

With his next breath, Tom remembered something Rose had said the night before. "Call me tomorrow, cowboy. I want to know how things go with moving in your dad."

He'd promised he would, and then he'd confessed that he was worried about leaving his dad in Montana. She'd responded with, "I just painted all the bathroom baseboards myself. You can handle whatever happens tomorrow. And the next day."

Strengthened by her faith in him, by her belief that he was strong and capable, Tom once again felt the peace that only came when he allowed his worries to wisp away.

"Here we are." Jace pulled into the driveway behind their mother's car and got out. He unloaded the wheelchair while Tom moved to open the door where his dad waited. With Jace steadying the chair, and Tom supporting his father, they managed to get their dad into the wheelchair without incident.

"You don't look good," Tom commented as he noticed the gray complexion of his dad's face. "You okay?"

He huffed and puffed. "I'm okay."

Tom exchanged a glance with Jace, and found the same nervousness in his brother's eye. "Let's get him inside."

"Let's lift him," Tom suggested when they came to the stairs. Every step, every bump, every movement elicited a groan from his father's lips. Even though Tom could tell Dad was trying not to complain, the pain he felt obvious. Tom winced with each stair, wishing he could take the pain from his father, remove this difficult recovery, shield him from this trial.

"There we go." Jace straightened, his face red. He wiped his palm down his face. "Okay." He turned toward the door, but not before Tom caught the weariness in his eyes.

Standing there, behind his broken father and seeing his exhausted brother, Tom knew for certainty that he needed to move back to Montana. Jace needed him. His dad needed him. And one glance toward where his mother stood watching, and Tom knew he could repair that relationship if he was here to do it.

He swallowed against the huge change, having just gone through packing, loading, unloading, unpacking more boxes than he could count. But he couldn't deny the feelings, couldn't deny that God wanted him to go home.

"Turkey sandwich." Tom set his dad's lunch on the couch next to him. The previous evening had passed uneventfully, as Dad had slept for fifteen hours after taking his prescription pain medication.

"How's your leg?"

"It's okay." Dad glanced up at Tom. "Thanks, son."

169

Tom heard the underlying vein of emotion. "Yeah, 'course." He returned to the kitchen and collected his own sandwich before settling into the armchair near his father. They ate in silence for a few minutes, while Tom worked up his nerve to speak.

"Dad," he finally said. "I'm gonna move up here."

His dad took precious seconds to set his plate aside and brush breadcrumbs from his hands. "Is that what you want?"

Tom nodded, sure in his decision. "Jace needs help. You need help. I want to help."

"Tommy, I want you to do what's important to you." Somehow when his father called him his childhood nickname, Tom wanted to smile and hug his dad, the man who'd raised him with love and hard work.

"Taking care of my family is important to me."

"You think you can leave your job in Texas? We know how hard it is when cowhands up and leave without warning."

Tom thought of Garth, of Ethan, of all his work for Pete and Courage Reins. "I have some loose ends to tie up," he admitted. He pictured Rose's beautiful face and kissable lips. "It might be a few months before I can get up here."

His father took a long drink from his water glass. "Take the time you need. I'll still be here." He flashed Tom a rare smile.

"There's another thing I wanted to talk to you about." He cleared his throat. "I've been seeing a woman in Texas."

"'Bout time," his dad said. "How serious is it?"

Tom took off his cowboy hat and ran his fingers through his hair. He didn't have time to say anything before his dad said, "Oh, about like that." He blew out his breath. "Well, maybe she'll come up with you in a few months."

An insane amount of hope dove through him. "You think I should ask her to?"

"Do you love her?"

Tom shrugged, unsure if he could articulate his feelings for Rose, especially since he'd only realized how much he cared about her that very morning.

"How did you know you were in love with Mom?" Tom asked.

His dad focused on something beyond Tom, something Tom assumed existed way in the back of his memories. "I just knew," he said simply. "When you know, you know." He peered at Tom, who squirmed under the heavy gaze.

"I know," he said. The wonder he felt at being in love combined with the sickness over how he was going to keep Rose in his life and live that life in Montana.

Tom drove straight to Rose's on Friday evening without calling her. He wasn't sure he'd be able to keep his idea contained, and he wanted to deliver his well-rehearsed speech in person. Through all the unpacking, the grocery shopping, the setting up of medication schedules, the family dinners, the promise to visit again before he moved up there, Tom had thought of nothing but Rose and Mari with him in Montana.

Every hour, every day he spent in Big Sky Country reminded him of how much he loved his home state. He'd spoken to the new foreman—his brother—about a job at Horseshoe Home, and he'd even gone to Silver Creek to talk to Owen.

Tom had opportunities in Gold Valley. He felt confident he could get a job, and he knew moving closer to his dad was the right thing to do. The only thing he didn't feel confident about was when he should move, and how he was going to tell Rose. Thus, he'd practiced for days the things he'd say.

We'd have a nicer place than you have here. Housing is cheap there, Rose.

Or *I already have two job prospects, and Gold Valley is a lot like Three Rivers. There are two banks, and opportunities for you there you don't have here, Rose.*

Or *I checked into their special needs schools, and there's an academy specifically for children with Autism. Mari would be fine there. Please, just think about it, Rose.*

Tom glanced down at his speedometer and realized he was going twenty over the speed limit. He eased up on the accelerator and went through his lines again.

We can get married here and then move there, maybe before school starts in the fall. I love you, Rose.

He paused his rampant thoughts at the idea that he loved Rose Reyes, the same way he had while unpacking his father's kitchen plates. It felt as real, as whole, as round, as wonderful, as confusing now as it had then.

She'd called a couple of times, and he'd put her off with a text a while later, claiming how busy he was. He just didn't want anything about how he felt, or the plans he was concocting to come through in his voice. And he didn't trust himself to speak to her until they could be face to face.

The minutes and miles marched by, and Tom pulled into her driveway just as dusk settled. He strode up the sidewalk and knocked on the door at the same time he opened it. The house sat in silence, except for a scratching noise from the dog kennel near the entrance to the kitchen.

"Rose?" he called, though he had a feeling she wasn't home. Despair speared him, stronger than he'd thought possible. In all his careful planning, it had never occurred to him that Rose might not be home.

"Mari?"

The garage door banged open and Mari stood there, tears streaming down her face. She locked eyes with Tom and screamed. Screamed louder than Tom knew a person could scream. Screamed longer than he thought an eleven-year-old had breath.

"Mari, honey, what's wrong?" he called over the sound of her rage. Tom was quite certain she was physically fine, and that the wildness in her eyes was due to anger and not pain.

"Dad's moving!" she shouted. "Marry that woman and Washington and—" She screamed again, this time running straight at him.

Adrenaline coursed through him and the only thing he could think to do was brace himself. She barreled into him and he caught her up and held her tight. She writhed against his chest, but he held her firm, whispering soothing words into her ear. It only took about a minute for her to quiet, and he smoothed her hair, realizing he loved Rose's daughter too. He felt her pain and anguish all the way down in his soul, and he ached that her father was moving so far away.

But Washington isn't that far from Montana, he thought, and he added it to the list of reasons why Rose simply had to marry him and move to Gold Valley by August. He didn't want his father to face the winter alone, and he could make sure he didn't leave Three Rivers in a lurch if they had a few months to make the transition.

"Come on, now," he soothed, lifting the girl and settling her on the couch beside him. "Tell me what's wrong, Mari."

Rose came through the door, her mouth tight and her eyes wet. She froze at the sight of Tom holding Mari, and their eyes locked for a single breath. She hung her head and continued into the kitchen.

Tom couldn't wait any longer. He lifted his arm from around Mari, his skin buzzing with nerves or excitement, he wasn't sure which. "Mari, can you stay here and watch TV? I need to talk to your mom."

She sniffled, switched on the TV, and changed the channel. Tom waited a few extra seconds to make sure she was completely settled before going into the kitchen.

"Rose."

She turned from her position at the kitchen window, her arms folded and her chin slightly wobbly as she obviously worked against the emotions trying to get out.

"You came back," she said, losing the battle against her tears.

Tom rushed toward her and gathered her into an embrace he hoped could say more than his words could. "Rose, my love, what's wrong?"

She melted into him, clung to him like she was drowning and he was her only support. As he held her and stroked her hair, he abandoned all his carefully practiced words, and went with, "I love you, Rose Reyes. Whatever's wrong, I'll fix it."

Chapter Thirteen

Through the echo in Rose's ears, she heard Tom say he loved her. Through the tears he wiped, she heard him mention moving to Montana with him. Through the whirlwind her life had become, she heard him ask her to marry him.

She pulled away as if he'd become electric, her brain trying to process what her ears had sent. "What are you saying?"

He fell back a step, his cowboy hat shading his eyes slightly. "I'm saying I love you, and want you to marry me and move with me to Montana."

She shook her head and gripped her elbows in cold fingers. "That's crazy."

"I know," he said. "I know it is. But you're all I thought about in Montana, and I—I have to move there. My family needs me, and God's calling me there. I know it's bad timing, and we're just starting...." He gestured between them, his eyes taking on an edge of desperation. "This. But it feels right, Rose. And it'll be closer to Ed, and Mari can still see him the way she does now, because Gold Valley is only a few hours from Washington." Tom paused to breathe, and she held up her hand so he wouldn't start again.

Rose's mind reeled and all she could do was blink. "Tom, I—"

"Don't say no," he said quickly. "I'll go, and you can think about it, and I'll see you out at the ranch this week for Mari's riding session, okay?" He swiped off his hat and handed it to her.

She took it, unsure as to why. She stared first at it, and then him as he stepped into her, gathered her close. So close she felt safe and comfortable, loved and appreciated. She felt everything she hadn't felt for so long. Everything she didn't get from anyone else. Within the circle of his arms, no cyclone could destroy. No earthquake could rumble.

She breathed in the woodsy scent of him, relished the fabric of his shirt against her check, and tipped her head back to kiss him.

Long after he'd left, the taste of him lingered in her mouth. The sound of his words floated in her ears. The lightness of his touch feathered across her skin.

But moving with him to Montana?

It was the craziest thing she'd ever heard.

Yet Rose couldn't sleep that night. She let Mari fall asleep on the couch, unwilling to invoke another episode, and she lay in bed, awake, thinking.

Did she love Tom Lovell?

She thought of his spiritual strength. His ability to fix things around the house, fix her, fix Mari. The image of him holding Mari while she sobbed, how quickly he'd been able to soothe her, ran circles through her mind.

She loved what he did for Mari.

She loved what he'd done for her.

She loved that he wanted to attend church, and do what the Lord directed him to do, and help his family.

But Rose knew she didn't love *him*—not yet—and she finally fell asleep with tears trailing down her cheeks.

Somehow Rose helped Mari get ready for school. She left her purse on the kitchen counter and had to go back, then she realized she'd never taken Paprika out before kenneling her, and went back a second time.

By the time they arrived at the academy, Mari was so late, Rose had to go into the office and sign her in. To top off her hectic morning, she had a client waiting in her office when she finally got to the bank.

"Sorry," she tossed to the bank manager and dropped her purse on the floor near her desk. "Good morning, Mister Phelps."

Minutes bled into hours, and then days, until Thursday came. Her heart wouldn't settle, and she couldn't stomach anything more than water as she prepared to take Mari out to the ranch for her therapy riding.

She'd surely have to see Tom.

Unless he asked someone else to do Mari's lesson. She seized onto the thought, but she couldn't bring herself to pray for the possibility. She wanted to see Tom again, feel his fingers in her, touch her lips to his. Maybe then she'd know what to do, what to say.

Because as she pulled up to the facility, she had nothing.

Sure enough, Tom lingered in the doorway of the barn, that cowboy hat pushed low over his midnight eyes so she couldn't read him. Her heart thundered now, causing a storm inside her chest that included lightning and wind and rain.

With every step she took closer to Tom, the storm raged more violently.

"Evenin', Mari." He reached for her hand. "How are you feeling today?"

"Good," Mari said. "Better. Ready to ride."

Tom smiled at her and turned to lead her through the barn. He didn't even acknowledge Rose, and an arctic wind knifed through her. She hugged her arms around herself, wondering if he could feel her indecision across the yards that separated them.

She turned to go up the stairs to the observer room, turning back when she heard him say, "Keep goin'. I need to talk to your mom for a minute."

He approached without hesitation in his long strides, slid his hands up her arms to her shoulders, and kissed her as a way of saying hello. She loved the strength in his arms, the tenderness in his kiss, the gentleness he used when handling Mari.

But again, something whispered through her that she could not accept his marriage proposal and move halfway across the country with him because he was kind to her daughter. She could not cheat him of a wife who loved him, simply because he could provide a sanctuary from the chaos her life had become, because he could calm Mari when Rose couldn't, because Montana was closer to Washington.

"We'll talk after, all right?" He didn't wait for her to answer before he turned and re-entered the barn. Rose climbed the steps to the observation room on shaky legs, knowing she only had an hour to order her thoughts into coherent sentences.

If only that storm in her soul would blow itself out so she could think straight. But it didn't when Mari progressed Peony into a trot, or by the time the session had ended. Tom sent her to brush down the horse, and Rose descended the steps to the barn.

Tom laced his fingers through hers and led her out into the night. The stars shone overhead, creating a magical, midnight blanket. When he looked down on her, she saw the same background in his eyes.

"I realize I sprung things on you," he said. "I'm sorry about that." He removed his gaze from her, and relief accompanied his words. She still didn't know what to say, but the words teemed just beneath her breastbone, and she knew they'd come out soon enough.

"I do feel strongly that I need to go home," he continued, his boots scuffing against the gravel behind the training facility. "I've spoken to Garth, and Pete, and Squire about it." He stopped and she paused with him. "They're just waitin' on me to tell them when I'm leaving."

He turned toward her, taking her other hand in his. "And I'm waitin' on you to tell me if you can come. It doesn't have to be now. Mari can finish the school year here. We can take all summer to get married and move. I know she's already upset about Ed and everything."

"She is," Rose choked out. "And I can't—" She shook her head. "I won't cause any more disturbances in her life right now."

"I understand, Rose." He pressed a kiss to her forehead and she leaned into his touch. "I just want to be in Montana before the winter, which, let's be honest, could start as early as September. I'm sure you'll want to be there before school starts for Mari. It's months away."

"Months," she echoed, seizing onto the prospect. She didn't have to love him now. She had months more to fall in love.

"How close is Gold Valley to Spokane?" she asked, instantly despising herself for the question. She couldn't marry Tom because it was convenient! Because it was close to where her ex-husband would be living.

"'Bout three and a half hours."

But three and a half hours was infinitely closer than a four-hour plane ride. Mari would be able to see Ed every other weekend, as she did now. If Rose stayed in Texas, Mari might get to see her father twice a year.

A battle ensued in Rose's mind, and she bit her bottom lip as she surveyed the wild range in the dark.

"Rose, I need a yes on this one," Tom said.

Rose looked up into his face. His handsome, honest face. She admired so much about him. All the chaos in her brain quieted. Only the evening wind could be heard, and Rose had the answer she'd sought for days.

"No," she said, her voice small yet strong. "I'm not ready, Tom, and Mari's not either."

He dipped his chin to his chest, released her hands, and stepped back. He started nodding and didn't stop. "Even with a few more months?" he asked, his voice low and strained.

"Maybe in a few more months." She touched his forearm. "But that's not fair to you. I can't have this be all about me."

Tom lifted his eyes to hers, stared right into her soul. He seemed to find what he needed, because he said, "Okay, let's get back before Mari can't find us and freaks out."

Friday morning, Tom knocked on Garth's door before the sun rose. He'd been up late, trying to formulate a new plan for when he should move, and if he should call Rose and beg her to reconsider.

A nagging thought in the back of his brain haunted him. One that spoke of his rashness, his quick decisions, his inability to think through possible outcomes before acting.

Stop it, he commanded himself. He knew the voice belonged to his ex-girlfriend, and he was tired of listening to it.

Garth opened the door, fully dressed and ready for the day. "Mornin', Tom. You want coffee?" He stood back from the door so Tom could enter.

Tom had already had two cups of coffee, but he entered the foreman's cabin and poured himself a third mug. "I've decided to leave at the end of the month."

Garth's eyebrows disappeared under his cowboy hat. "Really? Rose will be ready to move by then?"

Tom swallowed a searing mouthful of liquid, feeling the burn go up into his sinuses and down into his gut. "Rose isn't comin'."

Garth's face wilted into a sympathetic expression. "Tom, I'm sorry."

He waved away the apology. "It's okay. I mean, it's not like we're that serious." Tom felt a fool for even thinking Rose would feel as strongly about him as he did her. She had a special needs child, for heaven's sake. She couldn't simply uproot Mari, give up her job, her house, everything she'd built in Three Rivers, for a man she'd kissed a couple of times *two weeks ago*.

Still, his foolish heart pumped out an ache for her he couldn't name or contain.

"You're not?" Garth put his empty mug in the sink. "I thought you were."

Tom shook his head. "I asked her to come, but she said she couldn't. I understand her reasons."

"Do you?" Garth turned and pinned Tom with a calculating look. "Look, Tom, I know about love, okay? I was married once before, and what I see in your eyes when you so much as think about Rose…you love her. And she loves you too."

Tom stared at Garth, his mind not making it past his first confession. "You've been married before?"

Garth gave a single nod. "My wife died two years ago." A muscle in his jaw twitched. "I left Montana because I couldn't stand to be under that sky for another day without her." He stalked a step closer. "And I don't believe for a second you can go there without Rose either. Without her, that sky'll eat you up and spit you out."

"She doesn't love me," Tom said. She'd never said it, but he knew it to be true. If she did love him, she'd say yes. She'd finish the bathroom renovations and put her house up for sale. They'd get married in June, and go to Montana in July to look for somewhere to live. She'd visit the special needs school, and he'd find a job so they'd have what they needed come August when they arrived for good.

"She does," Garth assured him. "She just doesn't know it yet."

"That's the last of it," Tom said as he passed Pete on the steps. He lifted the dog crate into the front seat of his truck, where Winston would ride for the next two days as they made their way north to Gold Valley.

"You sure?" Pete peered through the open door into Tom's cabin.

"Yeah. Everything else belongs to the ranch. The next cowboy will need it."

Pete moved back down the steps. "I hate that you're leavin'. I mean, I know why you are, and I'm glad for you. But." He sighed and looked in the direction of Courage Reins, mostly concealed by the administration trailer and Tom's overly full truck.

"It's not gonna be the same without you."

"Who did you assign to Mari?" he asked. She and Rose come out to the ranch twice in the past month, but Tom had made sure he wasn't around. He didn't want to see Rose, because he knew he'd beg her to reconsider. And a fifth generation cowboy didn't beg.

"Lawrence has been working with her. She's resisting him, and she's backpedaled a bit." Pete glanced at him. "Don't feel bad. It happens. There's nothing you can do about it."

"Right," Tom said, trying to erase the guilt coating his tongue. Just like there was nothing he could do about the constant ache deep in his stomach, or the way he couldn't sleep for more than a few hours at night because he was worried he'd miss Rose's call telling him she'd sold her house and was waiting for him in Montana.

"Does she ask about me?" he asked.

"Rose?" Pete asked.

Tom shuffled his feet, wishing his neck didn't get so hot at the mere mention of her. "No, Lieutenant. Mari."

"All the time."

At least with Pete, Tom never had to wonder if he was telling the truth. He just wished it didn't hurt so much, cut so deep, echo so loud. "Okay, well, I better head out. I have to get all the way to Cheyenne today. It's eight hours."

"Good thing we got everything packed before breakfast." Pete clapped his hand on Tom's shoulder. "Come eat with us, then you can head out."

Tom headed over to Pete's house, his step light but his heart heavy. He'd had multiple confirmations over the past four weeks that moving was the right thing to do, mostly a peaceful feeling while listening to the pastor at church, or when Jace would call with updates about their dad's progress.

But he hated sitting behind Rose at church, so he'd started

leaving earlier so he could get a pew in front of hers. If he didn't see her, he didn't think quite so much about her.

He followed Pete into the kitchen, stopping when he found the entire space filled with people. All the cowhands, Garth and Juliette, and Pete's family crowded with several locals from town—Sandy and Vince and Reese and people Tom had known for the five years he'd lived in Three Rivers. A couple of his patients from Courage Reins sat in the living room.

His throat closed at the sight of them, all smiling and wishing him the best in Montana. He couldn't help looking for Rose, though he knew she wouldn't be there. He'd tried calling her a couple of times, right after she'd told him she couldn't move with him, didn't want to marry him, didn't love him.

He coached himself out of the negative space. She hadn't said all those things out loud, but as Tom had more time on weekends to think about where he'd gone wrong, what he should've done, his injured heart conjured up the implied meanings behind her saying she wasn't ready.

"Thank you," he told his friends. "I'm gonna miss you guys."

Chelsea drew him into a hug and whispered, "I invited Rose, and she said she really wanted to come, but just couldn't." She stepped back, then handed him a plate holding a Belgian waffle. He nodded that he'd heard and understood, but the pain knifing through his chest testified that he most certainly did not understand.

Breakfast ended too soon, though Tom knew he needed to hit the road. Today was the shortest day of driving, but he didn't want to go past Cheyenne until he knew what road construction he'd face through Wyoming and into Montana.

As the dust kicked up under his tires, Tom watched the other cowhands cross the parking lot from Pete's and get back to work. He stuffed away the guilt over leaving the ranch during the height of calf-tagging, with spring planting and branding right around the corner.

But he just couldn't stay on the ranch through the summer. These past four weeks had been torture enough.

He aimed the truck north, turning left when he almost always turned right. With his back to the town he'd loved, the town where the woman he loved lived, Tom remembered something he hadn't finished.

He groaned. "You never fixed Rose's car."

He'd never had time, and with every passing mile, he had the distinct impression that he'd never see her or Mari again. Especially because he knew her nearly-broken down sedan could never make the eighteen-hour drive to Montana.

Chapter Fourteen

"Where's your handsome cowboy boyfriend?" Fiona spoke with her Texan accent, her voice light, but Rose knew the question wasn't innocent.

"He moved to Montana," she said. "Remember I texted you about that?"

"Oh, did you?" Fiona stirred the baked beans on the stove.

"Yes, I did." Rose glanced at the timer on the birthday cake she was baking for Mari. Her daughter had turned twelve the previous week, but Rose always held a celebration for her on a weekend Fiona could come.

If Tom were still in town, he would've been there too. Rose knew it without question. He'd always been there, taking care of things, of her, of Mari, even when she asked him not to. One glance out the window and into the immaculate backyard, where Mari romped with Paprika, testified of that. A slow smoke rose from the pit in the corner, where Fiona and Rose had started a Dutch oven full of Kalua pork—Mari's favorite—several hours ago.

"I don't remember you saying anything about breaking up with him," Fiona insisted, causing Rose's blood pressure to reach nearly intolerable levels.

"Well, I did." Rose jumped as the timer went off. She shoved her hands into a pair of oven mitts and yanked open the oven. The scent of chocolate relaxed her a bit, though she wished it wouldn't. She'd gained five pounds this month as she tried to console herself with sweets. The weekends were especially hard, as she'd gotten used to Tom showing up every Saturday morning, that tool belt hanging dangerously low on his hips and a smile winking at her from under his cowboy hat.

The cake jiggled in the middle, and Rose slid it back into the oven for a few more minutes.

She turned toward her sister, who stared at her openly. "What?" Rose demanded.

"Tell me what happened with Tom."

"Fi—"

"Rose." She lifted the wooden spoon she'd been stirring with. "Big sister privilege. I get to know about all little sister break-ups."

Rose's shoulders drooped. "It hurts to talk about it."

"Mm hmm." Fi pulled a brick of cream cheese out of the fridge, along with a stick of butter. "But I knew about your forthcoming divorce from Ed before he did. You've always told me about your man troubles."

Man troubles paraded through Rose's mind. She hadn't had the best of luck with men, but trouble?

"And I haven't had a good story since the divorce, because

you've never dated anyone." Fi speared her with a look all big sisters must practice in the mirror before they go to bed. "So Tom must've been someone special, because he's the first man to even get you to go out with him."

"He is special," Rose admitted, sighing as she imagined his dark eyes, his strong arms, his gentle demeanor.

"So, naturally, you decided ending things with him would be better than being loved by a special man." Fi could make the desert in July sound appealing. It was why she was so successful as a real estate agent.

Rose rolled her eyes. "It's much more complicated than that. Ed had just gotten engaged, and he'd just accepted his new job in Washington." She looked back at Mari, who had settled down since Ed's move, though the change in assistants at Courage Reins had also added to her frustrations and emotional turmoil.

"I couldn't get engaged and move too. It's too much for Mari." She didn't mention that Tom had offered to wait until August. By then, Mari would've had plenty of time to adjust to Ed's engagement and relocation. Heck, she hadn't seen her father in three weeks, as he'd only had time to visit once before he moved to Washington.

"Mm hmm," Fi said again, pulling on Rose's last nerve. She hated when her sister hummed like that. It meant she didn't believe what Rose had just said. "I thought we'd decided you weren't going to make decisions based on Mari."

"I'm gonna go check the pork," Rose said and stepped out of the kitchen. She couldn't stand to continue the conversation with

Fiona—because this time her sister might actually be right.

Maybe the move to Montana—in August—wouldn't have been too much for Mari.

No, the truth was, everything Tom had proposed was too much for *Rose*. Too much. Too fast. Too perfect to be true.

"Evenin'." Pete met Mari as she got out of the car. Rose stood too, automatically glancing around for a cowboy she knew had moved a month ago.

"Evenin'," Mari echoed back to him. "Tom?"

"Tom's still gone, sweetheart." Pete took Mari's hand. "And I heard you had a birthday since last time I saw you. What are you now? Twenty-five?"

Mari laughed and went with Pete, who had taken over her lessons after she'd balked at Lawrence. "Twelve, Mister Pete."

"Oh, twelve." His low chuckle barely met her ears as they disappeared into the horse barn. Rose stared around the ranch, wondering when she'd started missing it so much. Driving here tonight, she'd felt the same giddiness in her stomach as the first time "Mister Pete" had invited her out to Three Rivers. She hadn't known then how much her life would change, how much it could improve.

Now, standing on the dirt road and watching another therapeutic riding lesson, and listening to her daughter talk to people, and with a dull ache in her heart for Tom, she realized how much Three Rivers Ranch had helped her.

Changed her.

Healed her.

"Evenin', Miss Rose."

Rose spun at the decidedly male voice, the twang so like Tom's she was sure he'd returned to Three Rivers. But Garth stood there, a half-smile on his face.

"It's a nice night," he commented, looking into the darkening sky. "Mari ridin' tonight?"

"Yeah." Rose nodded toward the outdoor facility behind Pete's house. "They went that way. I should go watch, but well...."

Garth shifted his feet. "Well, what?"

She shook her head, not sure how to finish the sentence.

"You miss Tom?" Garth's voice rose at the end, a genuine question.

Rose squirmed under the weight of his gaze. She understood why he was the foreman, why his cowboys obeyed him. She felt the same compulsion to tell the truth.

She sighed, steadfastly studying the prairie beyond the admin trailer and riding facilities. "Every day."

"You talk to him?"

She shook her head. "No, he hasn't called."

"You have a phone, right? It makes calls?"

Rose finally turned her eyes to his. He challenged her with a single raised eyebrow. "Well?"

"I'm afraid," she admitted, wondering if this man worked for Courage Reins, or simply possessed the ability to coax the truth to the surface.

"Of what?"

She shrugged, unable to articulate all her fears into a single sentence. Since Mari's birthday party and Fiona's humming fest, Rose hadn't stopped considering her options when it came to Tom. She'd thought about him day in and day out since he'd moved, but since the party, something had shifted. What, she wasn't sure, but she wasn't just missing him, or wishing he were in her house, fixing her sink or staining her cabinets.

But she was examining every possibility of how she might be able to see him again, what he might say, what she should do to make things right between them.

"I want to win him back," she said more to herself than to Garth. Her voice carried a measure of wonder, the same way the wind carried seeds to distant soils.

"Of course you do," Garth said. "You're in love with him."

She dropped back a step at his words. "No—No—I—"

"Love him," Garth supplied when she couldn't adequately finish the sentence. "It's okay to admit you love him."

Rose searched his expression, panic pouring into her bloodstream. "How do you know?"

"Know what? That you love Tom?"

She nodded, then shook her head. "No, yes. I mean, how do you know when you're in love?"

"You've been married before," Garth said. "So have I, so I know a little bit about bein' in love." He took a step closer, like he didn't want anyone to overhear what he was about to say. "You think about that person all the time. You wonder what they're doing, and if they're thinking of you. You recall all the good things about them, their best qualities. You think maybe you won't make it through the day without talking to them."

Garth shook his head, as if just remembering Rose stood there with him. "At least that's how I felt about Kim. Losing her——" He cleared his voice as it cracked. "Well, I wouldn't like anyone to go through that. Especially you, Miss Rose." He leaned into her and gave her a quick squeeze. "I kinda like you, and I know Tom is in love with you." He stepped back and started to move away. "Maybe call him?" he called over his shoulder as he moved between the admin trailer and the barn.

Rose watched him go, a warm feeling rising up her throat. It felt good to have friends, people who understood, people who didn't judge her and her poor decisions.

"My poor decisions," she murmured to herself. She spun, her hands flying to her throat. She needed to speak with Tom right now.

Tom exhaled heavily as he climbed into the cab of his truck. Ranching in Montana was a whole different ballgame. One he'd forgotten the rules of, one he hadn't played in too long. His shoulders ached, though he hadn't done anything today he hadn't at Three Rivers. But somehow, moving hay from the storage barn to the horse barn had taken twice as long—mostly because the tractor had gotten stuck in the mud.

Now that it was nearing the end of May, the melting snow had turned the landscape into a maze of dry spots and wetlands. Every chore seemed twice as challenging, and Tom wondered for the hundredth time if moving to Montana was the right decision.

As he drove the miles to his father's house, Tom knew it was. Montana was just different than Texas, and different didn't necessarily mean bad, or wrong.

"Dad?" he called as he entered the house. His father's injuries had healed considerably, and he'd started venturing outside the house to the yard, which he hadn't finished putting in last summer.

When he got no response, Tom moved through the kitchen and opened the sliding glass door. He stepped onto the deck and scanned the backyard. He couldn't see his dad, and Tom's heart rate spiked.

"Calm down," he coached himself. "He's probably in the shed." His father had built a shed on the edge of the yard, immediately behind the garage. He'd insulated it, put in an industrial space heater, and told his sons he was planning to spend his retirement making furniture. He'd hinted that he'd like to make rocking horses for his grandchildren, and Jace had joked that he hadn't been able to get engaged because *someone* kept falling. Tom had left the room, the thought of never seeing Rose again too much to handle in that moment.

He moved toward the shed, the soft warble of his dad's favorite crooners coming through the closed doors. Tom relaxed with the music, and the stars, and the way his breath hung in the air in front of him.

He knocked on the door as he opened it. A blast of heat licked his face, and he inwardly sighed. "Dad?" Glancing around the shed, Tom found everything in its precise place, much the same way as his father's cabin. His dad stood in the corner of the shed, face bent over a table saw that screamed so he couldn't hear Tom.

Tom closed the door to preserve the heat and waited until his dad cut the wood. "Dad," he said when the saw silenced. The scent of sawdust and earth filled his nose, reminded him of a simple life. A good life.

"Hey, Tom," his dad said over his shoulder. He went back to examining the wood, running a tape measure along the length of it and consulting a sheet of paper.

"Dad, we're meeting Jace and Wendy for dinner tonight, remember?"

His dad startled. "Is it that time already?" He glanced at the clock. "Shoot. Give me five minutes to clean up."

Tom couldn't help the grin that stretched across his face. "Sure, five minutes." He knew five minutes for his dad meant a half an hour. He reached for his phone to text Jace, so he'd know they'd be late. He didn't have it.

He patted down his pockets, but he didn't have it. He sifted through his thoughts, trying to remember when he last had it. Definitely on the ranch. He couldn't remember having it in the truck on the way here, but he'd had it in the hay barn and at his cabin, where he'd plugged it in while he showered.

An uncomfortable sensation writhed in his gut. He hated being without a way to communicate, and he especially didn't like driving from town to the ranch without his phone. He took a deep breath to calm himself. It was just a phone. No one but Jace messaged him, and he'd see his brother in a few minutes.

"You comin'?" his dad asked from the doorway, and Tom turned away from his thoughts.

"I left my phone home," he said as he stepped into the yard.

"I have one."

"You got a cell?"

His dad limped toward the back door. "Your mom badgered me about it long enough, and I was tired of listenin' to her complain about not bein' able to get ahold of me."

Tom's heart pinched at the mention of his mother, though he'd come a long way in rebuilding the bridge between them. Laura lived in Missoula, a couple of hours south of Gold Valley, and Tom had met her for lunch the first weekend after he'd moved to Montana.

As he'd eaten with his mom, he'd thought of Rose, and what he used to do on the weekends in Three Rivers. She'd noticed his melancholy disposition, but he'd put off her question about what was wrong. He didn't want to talk about his broken romance with his mother. He wasn't ready for that, and she didn't get to have a seat at that table of his life quite yet.

So he'd turned the conversation to his new cowboy cabin, which was really decades older than him and had been inhabited by a sixty-five-year-old man—his father—for forty years before he moved into it.

But it sat on the very edge of the ranch, a good two hundred yards from the other cabins—and he didn't have to share. A stand of trees bordered the back, and Tom felt like he had a real home as opposed to somewhere to sleep at night.

He'd installed floor to ceiling bookshelves in the living room and put up pictures of his family, his friends in Three Rivers, and his horses. Over the past couple of weeks, he'd started installing hard wood floors he'd rescued from the old barn and refinished—with the foreman's approval, of course.

Tom refocused his attention on helping his father up the back steps to his house. "Mom call you a lot?" Tom asked, not sure why he cared.

"A little bit."

Tom settled into his dad's couch while he went to get ready. He stared at the blank TV, thinking of Rose, and what she was doing. He wondered if she was staring at the TV while Mari watched her cartoons, thinking of him.

He sighed, closed his eyes, and wished this pain would vanish the way his muscle aches did. He wished he could take a pill and make the Rose-shaped hole in his life fill.

"All righty," his dad said, entering the room smelling like cologne. "I'm ready."

Tom heaved himself off the couch and mentally prepared himself to spend the next couple of hours with his brother and his new fiancée. He liked Wendy, he did. And he was happy for Jace, he was. But seeing them hold hands and laugh, conversing with them about their upcoming wedding, feeling their happiness only served to remind him of what he'd left in Texas.

On the drive to the restaurant, Tom contemplated calling Rose.

He'd thought about it constantly on the road through Colorado, and then Wyoming. By the time he hit Montana, he'd ruled it out as a possibility. He wasn't going to try to maintain a relationship with her from thousands of miles away, though he knew people did it.

She hadn't called either, and again, he wondered if she'd thought about it. If she wished he'd call. He probably should've at least called on Mari's birthday, but they'd lost three calves to a sinkhole that day, and he'd spent eight hours up to his neck in mud trying to get them out.

His fingers itched to fire off a text to her, see if she'd respond. He remembered he didn't have his phone as he pulled into the restaurant parking lot, and again, he forced himself to swallow down the rising desperation to sprint back to his cabin and get it.

Instead, he locked the truck and followed his dad up the steps, the tantalizing scent of steak overriding his circular thoughts of Rose, for once.

Chapter Fifteen

Rose dialed Tom's number again, this time securely shut behind her bedroom door. She'd called from the ranch, but he hadn't answered. She realized he was a time zone behind her, and possibly hadn't finished work for the day. She knew most cowboys left their phones at home during the day, using radios to communicate with each other while out on the range.

So she'd waited. Fed Mari a late dinner. Put her in front of the TV and retreated to her bedroom—where his phone rang and rang and rang.

Frustrated at the sound of his recorded voice—though the deep, smooth sound of it caused a ripple in her stomach—she hung up without leaving a message. She didn't know what to say anyway. He'd see her calls when he looked at his phone next, and she closed her eyes and sent a prayer to the ceiling that he'd call back.

She hauled herself off the bed and went to help Mari with her pajamas. If it were the weekend, she'd let her fall asleep on the couch, but they had to endure one more day of work and school tomorrow. Once she had Mari tucked safely into bed, Rose returned to her room and settled into the pillows. She stared at the ceiling, wondering where Tom was right now, and who he was with, and why he hadn't answered his phone.

She drifted to sleep with his handsome face in her mind's eye, the scent of the wind and his aftershave in her nose, the curl of his name on her lips.

Sometime later, she woke to the peal of her ringing phone. She scrambled for it, her heart sending shockwaves through her body. Her first thought centered on her parents—maybe something had happened. Then Fiona.

Then Tom.

His face brightened the screen, and Rose pressed her eyes closed for half a second before answering the call.

"Tom," she breathed, the sound barely leaving her lips.

"You called," he said, his voice as hushed as hers and filled with surprise.

"I did," she said. "Twice."

"Why? What happened?"

Rose cringed that he thought something had to happen for her to call him. It *had* been two months of radio silence on both ends.

"I—I wanted to hear your voice," she admitted. "I miss you, cowboy, and I was talking—"

"You miss me?"

"All day long." Rose sucked in a breath and held it. She hadn't actually articulated her feelings for Tom, not to herself, not to anyone. They still swirled beneath her breastbone in mysterious colors, emotions she couldn't quite describe.

"I miss you, too," he said. "Sorry I didn't answer earlier. I accidentally left my phone in my cabin and went to dinner with my family."

Rose seized the comfortable subject. "How's your dad?"

"He's recovering really well." Tom spoke in his usual tone now, his Texas twang still evident though he was a Montana cowboy now. Rose loved the rumble in his voice, the way he didn't waste words but still told a complete story.

"How's Mari?" he asked once he'd relayed that his dad could get around well enough, that his hip was nearly as good as he could expect.

"She's doing a lot better now that Pete took over her training," Rose said. "She still asks about you every time we go out to the ranch, though."

A pause came through the line, and Rose cursed herself for bringing up his absence.

"What are you telling her?" he asked. "Because I meant to call on her birthday, but we had an emergency on the ranch."

"You meant to call?"

"Absolutely."

Rose's heart grew two sizes, but she'd always loved Tom because of his care and affection for Mari. She'd already decided she couldn't marry him because of Mari. That she needed to love him because *she* loved him.

"Tom, I—will you call me tomorrow night, too?"

"I'll call you every night if you want me to." He cleared his throat, and she imagined him swiping his hat off his head and leaning down to kiss her. Her lips tingled in anticipation of it, though he lived so far away.

"Do you want me to call you every night, Rose?"

A smile burst onto her face as tears pricked her eyes.

"I need to hear you say yes, love."

"Yes," she whispered into the phone.

"Deal," Tom said. "Can I talk to Mari tomorrow too?"

"I think she'd like that."

"All right, then. I'll talk to you tomorrow. It's got to be pretty late there. Sorry, I just realized that."

"It's fine," she said. "But if you want to talk to Mari, you'll have to call earlier."

"How about eight?"

"Perfect."

"Perfect," he echoed, and Rose could hear a smile in his voice. "I love you, Rose. Thank you so much for calling."

"Thank you for calling back." Rose said good-bye and hung up, the three words she wanted to say to him still lodged in her throat.

"Tomorrow," she promised herself, snuggling into her pillow like it was made of pure down. Happiness roared through her and she felt warm from head to toe, because Tom had called back.

As she lay in bed, her eyes closed as she tried to fall asleep, a voice whispered through her mind. *Go to Montana and be with Tom.*

Rose dialed her sister the next day during her lunch break. "Fiona," Rose said after her sister answered. "I need you to listen to me very carefully, and not freak out, or talk, or interrupt until I finish."

"I'm insulted you have to give me such precise instructions for this conversation."

"No, you're not." Rose took a deep breath. "I need to sell my house, and I want you to do it."

Fiona started to squeal, and Rose shushed her. "I'm not finished yet. I need to sell it for probably more than it's worth. I need to be able to buy a new car. One that will get me and Mari and everything we own to Montana."

A giggle came through the line, and Rose gave her sister an immense amount of credit for her restraint.

"I need you to find someone in Montana that can show me some houses." Sudden dizziness swept over her. What was she doing? Moving so far away without somewhere to live, a job, anything?

She pressed her hand to her forehead. "I'll need your help talking to Mari about this change. And with the packing. And maybe making sure I don't back out of this completely."

The silence on the other end of the line unnerved Rose more than it helped. "I'm done now. Talk, Fi."

Fi didn't talk. She screamed—a happy, joyful, girlish type of squeal, like she'd just been asked to the prom by the boy of her dreams.

"So you love Tom," she said, and Rose couldn't deny the feelings any longer. She didn't want to, no matter how much they scared her. No matter how uncertain things in Montana would be. No matter how upset Mari might become.

"Yes," she said. "I love Tom."

Another shriek nearly deafened Rose, who pulled the phone away from her ear until her sister quieted.

"Have you told him?" Fi asked next, and Rose let her chin drop to her chest. "I don't like how long it's taking you to answer," Fi said. "But you must be talking to him again."

"I called him yesterday," Rose said. "He called back late last night, and—"

"Wait a second. *You* called him?"

"Yes."

"Why did you do that?"

"I missed him."

"You've been missing him for two months. What changed?"

Rose thought of the ranch, of Garth's advice, of the hole in her chest that seemed to shrink with the idea that she could talk to Tom again. She remembered how happy she'd been after his phone call last night, how peaceful she'd felt about moving to Montana as she drifted to sleep.

Those feelings hadn't disappeared, or lessened, by the time she woke in the morning. She'd busied her mind with school and work preparations, planning to start the moving process with this call to her sister at lunchtime.

"I decided to call him," she said, answering her sister's question about what had changed. "I wanted to hear his voice, and find out about his father, and if you hadn't interrupted me, I was going to say that it wasn't a big deal. We only talked for seven minutes, and he said he'd call again tonight."

"Seven minutes, huh?"

"Yeah, it was short, but—"

"You know exactly how long you spoke to the man. Are you timing our conversation too?"

Rose rolled her eyes, especially when Fi tacked a laugh onto the end of her sentence. "Yes, and it's getting too long," Rose said. "Will you help me or not?"

"Of course I'm going to help you!" Fiona harrumphed. "I'll come out to your place tomorrow and we'll do an appraisal. I'll take the pictures I need, and we'll get the house listed first thing on Monday morning."

Relief like Rose had never felt before cascaded over her, fell like a gentle rain against her conscience. "Thank you, Fi."

"All the home improvements Tom made will drive up the price of the house. You'll probably get enough for that car you want."

"I need to buy a few more things for the bathroom." Rose suddenly felt heavy—she'd finished the painting in the bathroom, but her eye for design paled in comparison to Tom's. A keen sense of missing filled her as she thought about what color the bathmat and shower curtain should be to go with the pale blue paint he'd chosen.

Sell the house, and you can be at his side everyday, she told herself as someone knocked on her office door.

"I have to go, Fi. See you tomorrow."

"I'll bring sweet rolls!" her sister called as Rose hung up and tried to erase the emotional conversation from her face so she could meet her next client.

Tom called Rose on Friday night at eight o'clock. Saturday too. Sunday as well. They spoke about his job on the ranch, and Mari, and what Pastor Scott had said during his sermon. Tom fell into a rhythm, one that was steady and comfortable. He woke early and went to work. By evening, his back hurt, but his step was light as he made his way down the dirt road to his cabin. The June sun had warmed up the landscape and dried out the mud, something for which he was grateful.

He made himself dinner, or he ambled over to Jace's to eat. He always made sure he was home at seven forty-five so he could gear himself up to call Rose. This pattern continued for a week, then two.

He told her he loved her, but he never asked her about coming to Montana. He never mentioned going back to Texas to visit. As the days passed, he wondered what he was doing. Was this their relationship now? Nightly phone calls without the promise of a real future together?

Dissatisfaction flowed through Tom as he headed out the door for another day of branding. Everything in Montana happened a bit later than in Texas, and Tom hadn't missed the dreaded chore after all.

The stink of burnt cowhide met his nose before he left his front porch, and Tom frowned though the big sky overhead shone with a blue he had never seen in Texas. He took a deep breath, set his shoulders, dismissed his thoughts of Rose, and pulled his gloves from his back pocket.

He thanked the Lord for this country, especially Montana, as he crossed over to the ranch and joined the other cowboys. He'd made a few friends in the nearly three months he'd been at Horseshoe Home, but no one was interested in driving into church with him on Sunday mornings. Tom missed Garth, though working for his brother was a comfortable gig he wouldn't give up easily.

Just like he hadn't given up Three Rivers without a pretty strong prompting from God.

"You comin' with us to the summer dance tonight?" Landon, a tall, tan cowboy who'd retired from the rodeo circuit last year, asked.

"Not much for dancin'," Tom said. He didn't want to hold anyone but Rose, and Jace had already told him that the cowboys were the first selected at the town dances held on Fridays throughout the summer.

He moved away from Landon discreetly, not willing to be drawn into a battle of why he couldn't go. He just couldn't. Surely Tom wasn't older than most of the cowboys at Horseshoe Home, but he felt decades more mature.

By the end of the day, he thought he'd never get the smell of hot metal and burning cowflesh out of his nose. He showered and stepped into the backyard to light his charcoal grill. One thing about working on a cattle ranch: There was always a lot of great beef to be eaten.

Something rustled in the undergrowth along the trees at the end of his yard. Winston lifted his head off his paws and sniffed the air.

"What's back there, boy?" Tom peered into the trees, but couldn't see anything.

Winston whined, stood, and took a couple of tentative steps toward the edge of the patio, his nose working overtime. Just when Tom thought he was about to spring toward the edge of the yard, he moved.

But not toward the trees. He tore around the side of the cabin, a bark flying from his mouth.

Tom covered the heating charcoal bricks and went to follow Winston. He hadn't heard anyone drive down the lane to his place. He rounded the corner, and sure enough, a dusty, blue SUV sat there. He didn't recognize it, but he knew it wasn't a ranch vehicle.

He heard a giggle form the front porch, and swung his gaze that way. Mari pushed at Winston's head, her laugh giving the dog the wrong impression about how she felt about him licking her.

She lifted her eyes and saw Tom, and she seriously pushed Winston back. "Tom!" She ran down the steps and across the yard, but Tom couldn't move.

Rose had turned from the front door when Mari had yelled his name, and their eyes locked. Seconds stretched into minutes as disbelief tore through Tom. Then Mari launched herself into his arms. Time rushed forward as he caught her and swung her around.

She laughed, and he couldn't help joining in. "What are you doin' here?" he asked her as he set her on her feet.

"We have a new life," she said.

Tom crouched in front of her, very aware that Rose lingered on the porch, her arms draped over the railing as she watched him interact with Mari. "A new life? What does that mean?"

Mari blinked her big brown eyes. "In Montana. We're going to live here."

Tom shot to a standing position, his legs carrying him toward Rose. She made him come all the way to the porch, where she waited with her arms wrapped around herself.

"What's she talkin' about?" Tom asked, not daring to believe the girl until Rose said the words herself.

She swallowed hard, the glint of tears in her eyes. "I love you, Tom Lovell." She swallowed again, and again. "I sold my house in Three Rivers, bought that car." She sniffled and pointed to the blue SUV. "I packed up everything I owned, and me and Mari drove to Montana." She took a step closer to him, a movement he catalogued though his brain spun, spiraled, spiked at all she'd said.

"We found a cute house in town," she continued. "And I have a job interview tomorrow."

Tom blinked, furious at his brain for not being able to tell his voice to speak.

She tiptoed her fingers up the front of his shirt, and he shivered at the touch he'd longed for.

"And I could use some help unpacking, so I thought I'd come out to the best ranch in Montana and hire me a handsome cowboy." She pressed closer and looked up through her eyelashes at him.

He still couldn't speak, so he did the only thing he could think of. He closed his eyes and kissed her.

Chapter Sixteen

Rose shifted her new car into drive with Tom beside her. Her nerves hummed with energy, with anticipation. For what, she didn't know. It had taken him five minutes to extinguish his grill and put Winston in the house, then he asked her to dinner.

Apparently unpacking could wait until tomorrow. Rose smiled as she turned back toward Gold Valley, her new home.

"Where are you interviewing tomorrow?" Tom asked, reaching across the console and taking her hand in his. He lifted her fingers to his lips, and a thrill squirreled down Rose's back.

"A mortgage company," she said. "Harward Finance."

"You want the job?"

"I *need* a job, and they need someone with loan experience."

"But do you want the job?"

Rose didn't understand. "It's not about wanting the job, cowboy. I have some money from the sale of the house, so we'll be okay for a couple of months. But I still need to find a job."

"I want you to do something you love. Not something just to make money." He frowned and glanced over his shoulder to where

Mari rode in silence. "I'm worried—"

"Tom, you don't need to worry."

"But I *am* worried," he said. "I don't want you to hate Montana."

"That would be impossible." She slid him a smile. "Have you seen the sky here?" She peered up through the windshield, appreciating how much Montana resembled Texas. Except for the mountains, of course.

"You haven't lived through a winter here yet," Tom grumbled, and Rose snapped her eyes to his.

"It snows a lot?"

"It snows and snows and snows," Tom said. "And the wind howls and howls and howls. And it lasts for a really long time."

Rather than worry over a season that sat months away, Rose focused her attention on the road, this one not quite as familiar as the one she'd driven so many times she had it memorized. She paused as she came to the four-way stop, suddenly unsure which way her house was.

"Um." She looked left and right before reaching for her phone. "I don't quite know where my house is…."

A moment of silence echoed in the car. Tom shattered it by laughing—a full belly laugh that sent Rose into a fit of giggles too.

"This town ain't that big, love." He took her phone and tapped a few times. "Oh, you live over by the old flour mill. I heard they built some new houses on that side of town." He nodded down the road. "Go straight."

Rose complied, and continued to follow his directions until she pulled into the driveway of a white house with navy shutters. The trailer she'd pulled from Texas sat in the driveway, much to her relief. She'd unhooked and set it herself, and she hadn't entirely trusted that it would be here when she returned.

She killed the engine and got out of the car, stretching her legs after the thirty-minute drive. She admired the lawn, though it needed greening up. She liked that an empty flowerbed waited for her personal touch. The pine trees on the west side of the yard provided some privacy, something she was grateful for when Tom slipped his arm around her and drew her into his side.

"We didn't stop for dinner."

"Can't work on an empty stomach?"

"Something like that." He held out his hand. "Want me to go grab something?"

"Sure, that would be great."

"What does Mari like?"

"Cheese quesadilla. And I want the biggest soda they have."

He pressed a kiss to her temple. "I can't believe you're here."

"Believe it, cowboy. And I hope you have your weekends free, because this house needs some serious remodeling."

Rose smoothed down her skirt and took a deep breath as the moment of her interview approached. Her foot tapped against the marble floor outside the senior partner's office at Harward Finance. The building felt impossibly clean, with secretaries stationed in precise places to help people get where they needed to go.

Rose liked the organization of it and she gripped her purse tighter. She'd driven Mari out to Tom's, because Rose didn't have anyone else to help with her. Tom didn't mind, Mari was certainly happy to spend time with the cowboy who'd completely captivated her the first time she'd met him.

"Miss Reyes?" a woman asked, and Rose tore her thoughts from her daughter. She glanced up and found the expectant face of the CFO.

"Yes." Rose stood and extended her hand. "Nice to meet you, Miss Keller."

The woman smiled and gestured for Rose to go ahead of her into the office. Rose's heart thudded against her ribcage, sending vibrations to her extremities. She took a calming breath as she sat across from a massive desk and waited for the other woman to walk around and take her seat.

She flipped open a folder she'd surely read a half-dozen times already. "So you were the loan manager at Three Rivers Bank? For almost ten years?"

"That's right," Rose said.

The woman closed the folder containing all of Rose's carefully documented experience and financial expertise. "Tell me, Miss Reyes. Why did you come to Montana?"

Tom's face filled Rose's mind, further anchoring her. "Well, let's see...."

On the weekend, Tom stood in Rose's living room, unboxing what appeared to be towels and sheets. He handed them to Mari, who took them down the hall to the linen closet. She returned like an obedient puppy and Tom handed her the empty box. She sliced the tape keeping it upright and folded the cardboard flat before tossing it into the pile by the front door.

He glanced around the house. It had an open floor plan, so he could see Rose working in the kitchen, stirring something on the stove that smelled heavenly. The dining room table held a half dozen open but unpacked boxes, and she turned from her task to go rummage through one of them to find what she needed.

She caught him staring as she turned back to the stove and gave him a brief smile. He returned it, noticing the curtain-less windows, the chipped countertops, the weathered linoleum. He wanted to race to the hardware store and buy everything he needed to make this house into a palace for the woman he loved. At the same time, he didn't want to complete a single project here.

No, he wanted Rose to come live with him out on the ranch. His renovation of the cabin was nearly complete, if he didn't count the basement that needed to be built from the foundation out.

"Have you heard from the mortgage company?" he asked to keep himself from blurting a marriage proposal. He'd included that in part of his speech about her moving to Montana with him, but nothing had been said since she'd arrived last week.

"Not yet," she said, keeping her back to him. "I got another interview somewhere else, though."

A slip of relief eased some of the tension he harbored in his neck. "That's great, love. Where?"

"Silver Creek." She turned to face him. "They need a new financial director there, and I applied today. They called a couple of hours later. Want me to come in tomorrow morning."

"Silver Creek?" Tom stepped around the couch toward her. "I went and spoke to their groom when I visited my dad, before I moved here." He reached for her, glad when she allowed him to draw her into an embrace. "You know it's a therapeutic riding facility, right?" He rocked from side to side slightly, the desire to hold Rose forever taking root in his very soul.

"Yes," she said. "I picked up some literature while I was there. It seems to be more for troubled youth than for someone like Mari, though."

"I know the groom. I can talk to him about using the horses for Mari. I can continue Mari's therapy. Silver Creek has doctors on staff." He gazed down at her. "She can have here what she had at Three Rivers."

Rose stretched up and kissed his cheek. "Maybe. We'll see how I feel after the interview tomorrow." She started to step away, but Tom tightened his hold on her, and she stilled.

He wasn't sure what he was doing, wasn't quite certain what he wanted to say. He swallowed past a dry throat. "Marry me," he said, refusing to look away from her.

She startled like he'd thrown cold water in her face with those two words.

"I don't want to fix up this house for you," he said. "I've been working on my cabin for a couple of months. It has two bedrooms and two bathrooms upstairs, and they're almost done. The basement is empty, and I'll build us whatever we want down there. I'll let you design it."

Rose grinned and gave him a playful push in the chest. "You know I can't design anything."

He chuckled and brought her closer before glancing over to where Mari sat on the couch with her tablet. "Mari, will you come over here?"

She swiped a final time and set her game down before coming toward them. He reached one arm around her too. "I just asked your mom to marry me. I want you guys to come live with me on the ranch." He watched her carefully, speaking a slip slower than he normally did. "What do you think of that?"

Mari blinked and looked at her mom. "Mom?"

"It's a thirty-minute commute to town," she said. "We'd have to get up early to get you to school."

"I can get up early."

Rose looked at Tom with such love in her eyes that a balloon of hope filled filled filled his chest. "I need to hear you say yes, love," he whispered.

"Yes," she said. "That's a yes, cowboy."

Chapter Seventeen

Rose slipped her feet into her slippers and padded down the hall to the kitchen. Mari snoozed on the couch, her typical bed on Friday nights. She didn't move as Rose started the coffee machine and checked her calendar for the day.

Cake tasting, dress fitting, and the final meeting with the wedding photographer. With the nuptials happening in only two weeks, Tom would spend the afternoon with Mari packing up the less essential things from Rose's house and moving them to his cabin on the ranch.

Her phone buzzed as the first drops of coffee fell into the pot, draping the house in the delicious scent of liquid caffeine. She glanced at the screen and found the face of Doctor Richards—the director of Silver Creek.

He'd sent a text that he needed the quarterly budget by Monday, instead of Friday as he'd previously said. Rose laid her head in her hands and groaned. She had time to finish the budget—it was almost done as it was. But she didn't want to do it today.

I'll get it to you first thing Monday morning. She took a steeling breath as she typed, releasing it as she hit send.

She loved working at Silver Creek. Tom and Mari could come with her later this afternoon, and while she finished the budget they could ride.

After she'd downed her first sips of coffee, Rose felt more like a normal person. She opened her computer and went to the guest list spreadsheet. Chelsea had called yesterday and confirmed that they were coming. Tom's brother, Jace, had offered the huge bunkhouse on the ranch for guests, and Rose added Pete, Chelsea, and their daughter Julie to the list.

Rose's parents were coming. Fiona and a plus-one she wouldn't give anything details about. No matter how whiny Rose became, Fi steadfastly refused to tell her who she was bringing to the wedding.

Squire and Kelly Ackerman, the owners of Three Rivers Ranch and Tom's longtime friends, were coming with their son, Finn. Kate and Brett had sent their congratulations, but due to Kate's pregnancy, they couldn't make the trip from North Carolina.

Garth had confirmed his seat, and he had a plus-one Rose wondered about as well. She hadn't asked him, hadn't spoken to him much after he'd helped pack her house and sent her on her way to Montana. She'd thanked him for his honest and heartfelt words, and wished him the best in finding his next love. He'd said nothing of Juliette, of dating someone new. Yet, he'd responded with a plus-one.

Rose smiled just thinking about who it would be. Mari stirred, and Rose turned toward her. She settled back to sleep, and Rose returned to her spreadsheet.

Tom's parents would be in attendance, but they didn't need accommodations. Rose's did, as they were coming all the way from Dallas. She'd put them in her house, though, instead of a bunkhouse with a dozen other people. Fi was staying here too, as Rose had paid rent through the end of August, and the wedding was taking place on the third weekend.

Only a week later, Mari would start at her new school, and the wave of worry that came whenever Rose thought about it pressed against the mouthful of coffee she tried to swallow. Tom had assured her that Mari had adjusted to Montana well, that she would be fine at the new academy. But still Rose worried.

Her phone buzzed again, a reminder that she had to be ready to slip into her wedding dress in only an hour. She left her coffee mug on the counter and went to shower.

The hours, days, and weeks slipped by until Rose woke on the morning of her wedding day. Her parents had arrived two days ago, and she heard someone moving around in the kitchen. Probably her father, who hadn't slept past four-thirty in a decade. Fi slept in Mari's old room, her ne man-friend down the street in a hotel. She'd simply introduced him at Derrick, a real estate photographer. There hadn't been much time to get details, but Rose had already scheduled a reminder in her phone to text Fiona about her new boyfriend.

Rose stayed under the covers, a smile creeping across her face as she thought about what today held for her. A second chance. A new life. A father for her daughter.

Gratitude overwhelmed her and she let the tears trickle down her face as she thanked the Lord for His care, His mercy, His guidance.

Fi banged on the door just as Rose wiped her face and sat up. "Time to get up, sleepyhead. I can't work my magic on your hair if you're lying on it." She grinned, a new sparkle in her eye as well, one Rose suspected had appeared because of Derrick.

Rose showered, and Fi braided, and their mother buttoned Rose into her party dress. The wedding dress waited for them in the bride's room at the church. After the ceremony, the reception would take place at Horseshoe Home, with Jace providing a steak dinner and some of Tom's new cowhand buddies putting on a real country ho-down for the dancing.

Nerves swept through Rose as her father pulled into the church parking lot. She wasn't sure if she was anxious or excited. Either way, her stomach felt like she's swallowed live snakes.

Chelsea and Kelly waited in the bridal room, ready with their makeup brushes. Rose sat still as they worked their magic, as her mother helped her into her gown, as the photographer took shots of all the key moments.

Her wedding with Ed hadn't been anything like this, though she'd had the perfect dress, her friends and family nearby, and someone to document it all. But the level of excitement in the air hadn't been present, and she wondered if she should've known that she and Ed weren't going to work out.

She shook away the negative thoughts, determined not to dwell on the past on her wedding day. She slipped into her heels just as Mari entered the room. She wore a pale blue dress that played well with her dark eyes and honeyed complexion. She smiled at Rose and wrapped her arms around her in a genuine hug.

Tears sprang to Rose's eyes, and she pressed them closed to keep the water from ruining her makeup. "Love you, baby," she whispered into Mari's hair.

"Love you, momma."

Rose sucked in a breath at Mari's sentiment, something she rarely expressed. They linked arms as they left the room, and then Mari went ahead with Rose's mother and the other ladies. Rose waited in the hall with her father, her fingers feeling numb though the August weather put up a good fight against the church's air conditioning.

"You ready?" Her dad looked at her, and she saw love reflected in his eyes.

"I'm ready."

The organ switched to the wedding march, and he offered her his arm. Rose took it before focusing her attention forward. Forward to the new life she was about to enter. Forward to a new family. Forward to a better future.

She took a deep breath and took the first step.

Tom waited at the front of the chapel, every nerve in his body at attention. The time for the wedding to begin came and went. He exchanged a glance with Garth, who'd brought a dark-haired woman with him to the wedding.

Tom hadn't had time to find out who she was. Juliette had decided to fly in last minute, and he'd spent the morning trying to find someone who wasn't busy to go pick her up from the airport. He barely recognized his aunt, what with her new bottle-blonde hair. She wore dark sunglasses, even inside the chapel, and Tom couldn't help feeling like something with her wasn't right.

He raised his eyebrows at Garth, who pressed one palm toward the floor, his sign for, *Be patient. She's coming.*

Tom wanted to ask Garth about Juliette, question him about the woman he'd brought instead of Juliette, interrogate him about why he kept staring at his aunt longingly when he'd come with a woman that wasn't Juliette.

The organ switched from it's gentle prelude to the wedding march, and Tom turned to the back of the hall, his heart bobbing up and then back to it's rightful place inside his chest. Watching Rose walk down the aisle with her father made Tom's insides liquefy. A sudden, strong responsibility to take care of her, to love her, to cherish her, descended upon him. Once she was passed to him, the ceremony blurred. He remembered the kiss, just as every kiss with Rose had been etched into his mind.

Over the past seven weeks as she planned the wedding and started a new job, Tom had tried to watch for signs of exhaustion or attitudes that suggested she was overwhelmed. He'd taken her flowers for no reason, showed up to mow her lawn on weekends, anything he could think of to show her he loved her and would take care of her and Mari.

He'd kissed her as often as possible, sometimes in her garage while Mari was in the backyard, sometimes she'd let him stay late after Mari went to bed, sometimes he'd send Mari over to the stables so he could kiss Rose in the privacy of his backyard.

A cheer went up from the crowd and Tom refocused his thoughts on more appropriate things. He ducked his head and rushed with Rose—his wife—down the aisle amid laughter and applause and a showering of rice.

They burst into the brutal Montana summer, where his truck waited. The engine rumbled and someone had tied streamers to the back bumper. Tom helped Rose into the cab, tucking her dress in as she laughed.

He leaned down and gave Mari a kiss on the cheek. "Go with Fiona, okay, baby? We'll see you out at the ranch."

Mari nodded and Tom hurried around the front of the truck to join Rose. She'd rolled her window down and was waving to her friends and family who'd come to celebrate with them. He admired her strength, her unmatched ability to coordinate details of a massive event while working, unpacking and then re-packing, dealing with Mari's new school, and ironing out a visitation schedule with Ed.

Tom reached over and took her hand in his. "Come sit by me, love."

It took some effort for her to scoot across the seat in her wedding dress, but she finally managed it. He lifted his arm and tucked her into his side, where he wanted her to stay forever.

"I love you, Rose," he whispered into her hair, and a feeling of peace and comfort settled across his shoulders.

"Love you too, cowboy."

The End

Read all the books in the Three Rivers Ranch Romance series!

Second Chance Ranch: A Three Rivers Ranch Romance (Book 1): After his deployment, injured and discharged Major Squire Ackerman returns to Three Rivers Ranch, wanting to forgive Kelly for ignoring him a decade ago. He'd like to provide the stable life she needs, but with old wounds opening and a ranch on the brink of financial collapse, it will take patience and faith to make their second chance possible.

Third Time's the Charm: A Three Rivers Ranch Romance (Book 2): First Lieutenant Peter Marshall has a truckload of debt and no way to provide for a family, but Chelsea helps him see past all the obstacles, all the scars. With so many unknowns, can Pete and Chelsea develop the love, acceptance, and faith needed to find their happily ever after?

Fourth and Long: A Three Rivers Ranch Romance (Book 3):
Commander Brett Murphy goes to Three Rivers Ranch to find some rest and relaxation with his Army buddies. Having his ex-wife show up with a seven-year-old she claims is his son is anything but the R&R he craves. Kate needs to make amends, and Brett needs to find forgiveness, but are they too late to find their happily ever after?

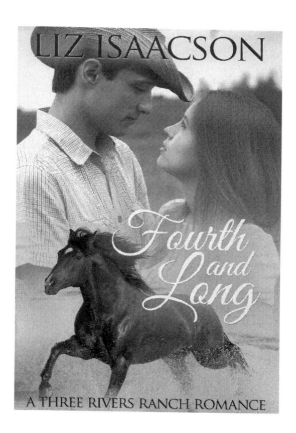

Fifth Generation Cowboy: A Three Rivers Ranch Romance
(Book 4): Tom Lovell has watched his friends find their true
happiness on Three Rivers Ranch, but everywhere he looks, he
only sees friends. Rose Reyes has been bringing her daughter out to
the ranch for equine therapy for months, but it doesn't seem to be
working. Her challenges with Mari are just as frustrating as ever.
Could Tom be exactly what Rose needs? Can he remove his
friendship blinders and find love with someone who's been right in
front of him all this time?

Sixth Street Love Affair: A Three Rivers Ranch Romance Novella: After losing his wife a few years back, Garth Ahlstrom thinks he's ready for a second chance at love. But Juliette Thompson has a secret that could destroy their budding relationship. Can they find the strength, patience, and faith to make things work?

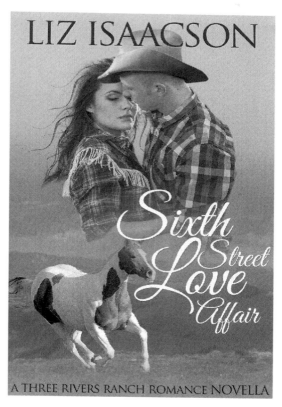

Get this digital-only novella for FREE when you join Liz's newsletter.

**The Seventh Sergeant: A Three Rivers Ranch Romance
(Book 5):** Discharged from the Army and now with a good job at
Courage Reins, Sergeant Reese Sanders has finally found a new
version of happiness—until a horrific fall puts him right back
where he was years ago: Injured and depressed. Down-on-her luck
Carly Watters despises small towns almost as much as she loathes
cowboys. But she finds herself faced with both when she gets
assigned to Reese's case. Do Reese and Carly have the humility and
faith to make their relationship more than professional?

Eight Second Ride: A Three Rivers Ranch Romance (Book 6): Ethan Greene loves his work at Three Rivers Ranch, but he can't seem to find the right woman to settle down with. When sassy yet vulnerable Brynn Bowman shows up at the ranch to recruit him back to the rodeo circuit, he takes a different approach with the barrel racing champion. His patience and newfound faith pay off when a friendship--and more--starts with Brynn. But she wants out of the rodeo circuit right when Ethan wants to rejoin. Can they find the path God wants them to take and still stay together?

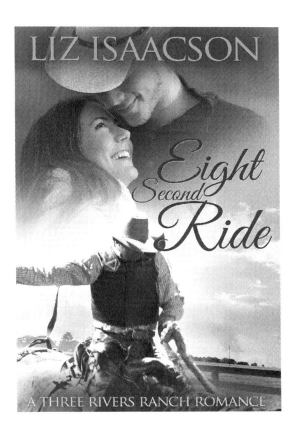

Read on for a sneak peek at the first chaper of *The Seventh Sergeant*, Book 5 in the Three Rivers Ranch Romance series!

Chapter One

The sky surrounding Carly Watters had never seemed so wide, so blue, so threatening. Of course, she hadn't set foot outside the city in half a decade. Her heart pulsed out an extra beat as she made a right turn and faced yet another two-lane highway without a single soul in sight.

The previous veteran care handler, Lex, had told her Three Rivers Ranch was another forty minutes north of town. Carly had half-thought she'd been kidding. But now, with her orchid satin heels pressing against the accelerator and the minutes ticking by, she realized Lex hadn't exaggerated at all.

Dismay tore through her when her tires met dirt road instead of asphalt, and she knew her shoes wouldn't survive more than a couple of steps in the dust and gravel. She'd bought the heels as a graduation gift for herself when she'd finished her social work Master's degree at TCU a couple of years ago, and they remained the most expensive piece of her wardrobe.

"This is a good job," she breathed to herself as that wide-open sky continued to suffocate her. "It's a promotion—one where you can afford to buy another pair of three hundred dollar shoes. So what if you have to come out to the sticks every couple of weeks?

It's going to be fine."

But as she pulled her cute, compact car into the parking lot next to a newer building, a sinking sensation in her stomach spoke that nothing would be fine. Carly pulled up the zipper on her jacket and reached for the file of the veteran she'd come all the way out to this ranch to see: Reese Sanders.

A Sergeant, Reese had suffered massive core injuries from a tank bombing a few years ago. Carly had already poured over Lex's notes, and she expected to find a "happy-go-lucky veteran who left his wheelchair behind after endless hours of horseback riding."

After she'd read his file, Carly had admired his tenacity, the way he'd clawed himself back from the edge of physical devastation. She'd had a taste of that kind of heartache in her life too, but it was bitter in the back of her throat and she painted over it with a fresh layer of lipstick and a smile almost as bright as the near-spring sun.

One of her mother's adages sprang to her mind. *Comparison is the thief of joy.*

Carly had tried to make the words mean something in her life, but with two Mary Poppins Practically Perfect in Every Way older sisters, and a twin sister that Carly was technically older than, she'd never quite been able to measure up.

Even her choice of social work—of dedicating her life to helping others—had been overshadowed by her twin's acceptance into a Ph.D program.

She locked her car as she clicked across the blessedly paved parking lot, the familiar *ba-beep!* somehow strengthening her to carry out this meeting in her usual cheerful manner. The wind caught her hair and blew the blonde locks around her face. She scrambled for the door handle, the weather pulling at her skirt, her jacket, her file.

Almost like God had pressed the fast-forward button on her life, the wind ripped the folder from Carly's grip. The folder containing all of Reese's accomplishments. The folder the previous handler had warned her not to misplace or rearrange. The folder that symbolized the beginning of what was sure to be a glorious, new career.

The weather snatched at the pages, sent them twirling through the air, and Carly could do nothing but watch. All at once, her life resumed its normal pace—all except her pulse, which thundered at four times it's normal speed. She swiped for the pages with her hands, stomped on others with her precious heels, even hipped one into the doorjamb to keep it from getting sucked into the open Texas range, never to be seen again.

As she attempted to gather together what pages she could, the crunching of paper behind her attracted her attention. She turned, hoping for a handsome cowboy with exceptional lassoing skills.

She'd hit the bullseye with the handsome cowboy bit, and she straightened, forgetting about the need to keep her hip curved into the building.

"Let me help you." He bent to grab a fistful of papers before they could be tornadoed away. When he straightened, his dark eyes sparkled with a smile, causing Carly's chest to squeeze in a good way.

"That must be your purple car." He nodded his cowboy hatted

head toward the parking lot.

Her defenses rose. "I like purple."

The man drank in her orchid heels. "Obviously."

"It gets good gas mileage."

"I'm sure it does." He took a couple of stunted steps forward, his hand outstretched, and understanding flooded her. "I'm Reese Sanders. What can I help you with?"

Instead of answering, she reached for his hand and catalogued the thrill that squirreled down her spine at the contact. Warmth from his skin bled into hers, and she allowed her lips to curve upward. "I'm looking for you, Sergeant Sanders." With a measure of regret she didn't quite understand, she withdrew her fingers from his. "I'm your new veteran care coordinator, Carly Watters."

"Ah." He glanced down at the papers again before pushing them toward her. "These must be Lex's notes." Reese shuffled backward, and it looked like he might fall. Carly automatically reached out to steady him.

The death glare he gave first to her hand on his forearm and then which he speared straight into her eyes left zero doubt about how he felt. She yanked her hand back, heat rising through her chest to her cheeks.

"S-sorry," she mumbled, her pinpoint heels suddenly too small to hold her weight. She sagged into the building again, not caring that it slouched her figure, despite her mother's warning voice in her head. "Can we go in and talk? You were expecting me, right? Lex told me—"

"I've been expectin' you, yeah." He bent and collected a paper stuck against the glass, handed it to her, and entered the building before holding the door open for her. "We can talk in the conference room." He nodded to the right. "Through there."

Carly took a deep breath as she passed him, not because she wanted to get a better sense of his smoky, spicy scent, but because she needed the extra oxygen to settle her nerves. Hadn't she read that Reese resisted help? That the only reason he'd even signed up for services was because someone else had called first?

Once inside the conference room, Carly shoved the papers back into the folder, intending to sort through them and put them back in order when alone. She didn't need him to witness first-hand her OCD when it came to her client's files. She moved to the head of the table and sat down.

"So," she started. "Tell me about your job here."

Reese closed the door and moved to the chair next to hers. He possessed a fluidity in his injury, something Carly hadn't expected. She admired the dark stubble along his jaw and found herself fantasizing about what it would feel like against her cheek. If his lips would be soft in comparison as they touched hers.

Her hand flew to her mouth as she sucked in a breath. She needed to find her center, stop this ridiculous train of crazy thoughts. Reese was a *client*. A veteran she was supposed to help. Nothing more.

"I'm the receptionist here at Courage Reins." Reese spoke with quiet authority, and another traitorous trickle of delight made her skin prickle.

"I answer phones, make appointments, help with the horses.

That kind of stuff."

Carly pulled out a random piece of paper from the folder and flipped it over. She clicked her pen into operational mode and wrote something. What, she didn't even know. She just wanted to look official, like she knew what she was doing. "You live in Three Rivers?"

"Yeah."

"You drive out here everyday?"

"Everyday I want to get paid."

Carly glanced up from her chicken scratch at the gruff amusement in his voice. His dark diamond eyes studied her, unsettling her and making her next question abandon her mind. Heat rumbled through her stomach, rising until it settled in her face. She shoved the useless notes back into the folder. "What can I help you with Sergeant Sanders?"

He leaned away from the table, his injury nowhere near his impressive biceps. The biceps that bulged as he crossed his arms and continued watching her with those gorgeous eyes. He seemed to be able to see right through her pretended professionalism.

"I don't need help," he said. "I'm doin' great. That's what I told Lex."

"It's procedure when a new care coordinator—"

Reese lifted one hand, rendering her silent. "I know," he said. "I get it. But I don't need anything right now. I'm good."

Oh, he was. Carly licked her lips and pressed them together, a slim vein of frustration sliding through her. She'd driven two hours for him to tell her he was good?

"Well, maybe I can get some groceries for you on my way back through town."

"I do all my shopping online."

Her eyebrows shot up. "You do your grocery shopping online?"

"You say that like I don't know how to use a computer." A deep chuckle accompanied the words. "It's easy, Miss Carly. You just login to this app, order what you want, and show up at the store." He dug in his pocket and extracted his phone, like he'd school her on how to order groceries online. "They bring everything right to me. I don't even get out of my truck."

Of course he'd drive a truck. Probably one of those huge, obnoxious pick-ups that she could never see around. Still, she wanted to hear him say *Miss Carly* over and over in that smooth, Texan twang.

She cleared her throat and straightened the already-neat file. "You sure there's nothing you need? I could stick something in the oven, start a sprinkler, get your mail—"

His arms uncrossed and his left hand came down on hers. "Miss Carly, I don't need anything. But if you wanted to hang around here for a while, I could show you the horses."

Panic streamed through her, mixing with a wild thread of joy at his touch. She could hardly sort through how to feel, not to mention what to say.

Finally, her mind came up with *He needs company*. And she could give him that, if nothing else.

"I—Okay," she said. "But I don't think I've ever seen a horse up close."

He looked at her like she'd just said she wasn't human. "Well, Miss Carly, that simply won't do." He pushed against the table and stood. Carly noticed the weakness in his core, the difference in length between his left leg and his right. Even with his injuries, he stood a few inches taller than her and radiated power and confidence as he reached the door and opened it.

Reese paused on the threshold. "Well? Come on. You can't leave Three Rivers without seeing at least one horse."

Reese had no idea why he'd invited Carly Watters to stay out at the ranch and see the horses. Even more surprising was that she'd agreed. He'd watched her war with something within, but in the end, she'd said yes.

Why'd you ask her at all? he wondered for the fifth time as he stepped onto the dirt road that led to the horse barn. He didn't know. But he did like her bright, blue eyes, her platinum hair, her purple car.

"So tell me about you," he said. "I'm sure that file gives you all my details."

"You have six older brothers," Carly recited. "From Amarillo. Served two deployments." Her voice caught on the last word, and Reese slid her a glance. She seemed mortified by what she'd said.

"I know I served in the Army," he said. "I know I got hurt. It's okay to talk about."

"Is it?" She peered at him like she wasn't really sure.

"Yeah, sure." Lex had assured him that her replacement was

amazing. That she'd take good care of him. Reese didn't need a lot now that he'd gotten the job at Courage Reins, now that he'd signed up for online grocery shopping. But he missed Lex. She'd always been good company for him. He wondered if his file said that.

Lonely. A sad, lonely veteran whose best friends have four legs and long manes. Or are already married.

"How long have you been a care coordinator?" he asked, glad when his voice didn't betray any of his emotions.

She gave a nervous giggle. "This is my first appointment." She froze on the gravel, and he thought she'd hurt herself in those bright heels. "I'm totally doing it wrong, aren't I?"

Reese retraced his steps back to her and hooked her elbow in his. "'Course not, Miss Carly. You're keeping me company, and that's exactly what I need right now."

She gazed up at him, and Reese's mind went into a tailspin. His pulse followed suit, and he forced himself to look away so he wouldn't say or do something stupid. He took a slow step toward the barn, relieved when Carly came with him.

He hadn't dated anyone since he'd come home broken, three years ago. Hadn't even thought about it. Had told Chelsea no over and over when she suggested women he could take out. But now, with Carly's cold fingers pressing into his forearm, he thought maybe he was ready to take a step toward getting to know her.

"So, you?" he asked. "I do have six brothers, and they're all married and successful. Does my file say that? That I'm seventh best? The seventh sergeant in the family?"

She shook her head, her loose curls brushing his arm. Fireworks tumbled up his arm and sparked in his shoulder. He hadn't felt like this about anyone for so, so long. He hardly trusted himself to know what it meant.

"No, your file lists your family stats, but nothing about them. Where are they?"

Reese took a deep breath as they stepped out of the weak sunshine and into the barn. Just the presence of animals settled him. "You're not getting out of telling me about yourself." He led her past the first stall, heading for Elvis. He clucked his tongue and the black-and-white paint stallion came trodding forward.

"Oh, he's gorgeous," Carly breathed as the horse lumbered toward them.

Reese let Elvis snuffle against his hand. "He's a thoroughbred. Won a few races before he hurt his leg." He spoke with love and reverence about the horse. "I rescued him from death. When a racehorse can't race...." He let the sentence hang there, grateful the gentle animal hadn't lost his life.

He'd been saved, the same way Reese had. Though he'd struggled to find worth inside himself, he saw it in Elvis, and he knew God had rescued them both. It had taken Reese many long months to get to that place, and a sense of gratitude filled him.

Elvis eyed Carly, and she shrank behind Reese. "Oh, come on, Miss Carly. He won't bite."

"He's taller than I thought."

Reese turned around. "Let's go see Tabasco. He's smaller."

She went with him, sure and strong on such skinny heels. "Who

names the horses?"

"Whoever owns them as foals. We don't get a lot of those here on the ranch. Our horses are either working horses or retired horses we use for therapy." Further down the line, Tabasco waited with his head already over the fence.

"See? He's much smaller."

Carly reached hesitantly toward him, and Reese willed the red bay to behave. He did, his eyes falling halfway closed as Carly stroked his cheek.

"He likes you."

Carly beamed under the compliment, and Reese wanted to make her feel like that again. "So, your family?"

"I have three sisters. Two older, and one twin, who I'm four minutes older than."

"A twin, huh?"

"Mirror twins," she said. "My hair parts on the left, hers on the right. I have a dimple on my left cheek, hers is on the right."

Reese had no idea what mirror twins meant, but before he could ask more, she said, "Basically everything Cassie does is right, while everything I do isn't."

He heard every syllable of resentment, of frustration, of sadness in her statement. In her next breath, she put on a happy smile and started asking him about the different breeds of horses.

Reese obliged and kept the conversation light and flowing. But he couldn't shake the feeling that maybe Carly Watters was as lonely as he was.

About Liz

Liz Isaacson writes inspirational romance, usually set in Texas, or Montana, or anywhere else horses and cowboys exist. She lives in Utah, where she teaches elementary school, taxis her daughter to dance several times a week, and eats a lot of Ferrero Rocher while writing.

Find her on her website at lizisaacson.blogspot.com.

She also writes as Elana Johnson, who is the author of the young adult *Possession* series, the new adult futuristic fantasy *Elemental* series, and two contemporary novels-in-verse, ELEVATED and SOMETHING ABOUT LOVE. Her debut adult fantasy, ECHOES OF SILENCE, was published by Kindle Press in May 2016. Her debut contemporary romance, UNTIL SUMMER ENDS, will be published by Cleis Press in 2016.

17032251R00149

Printed in Poland
by Amazon Fulfillment
Poland Sp. z o.o., Wrocław